DRAGON'S LAIR

The marriage of Davina and Gethyn Lloyd had been brief and disastrous, and they had not met for two years. Now circumstances had thrown them together again—and Davina knew that her feelings for Gethyn, far from fading, were stronger than ever. But how could she ever sort out the tangle of misunderstanding that still lay between them?

DRAGON'S LAIR

BY

SARA CRAVEN

MILLS & BOON LIMITED
17-19 FOLEY STREET
LONDON W1A 1DR

First published 1978
Philippine copyright 1978
Australian copyright 1978
This edition 1978

© Sara Craven 1978

ISBN 0 263 72726 2

Set in Linotype Lectura 10 on 10½ pt

Made and printed in Great Britain by
Richard Clay (The Chaucer Press), Ltd., Bungay, Suffolk

CHAPTER ONE

IT was rather stuffy in the small room. The air was heavy with the scent of ageing leather, paper and old-fashioned furniture polish—none of them unpleasant in themselves but oddly oppressive when served up in such a rich mixture. Or was it simply her over-charged emotional state which made them seem so? Davina Greer could not be sure.

She pressed her tongue over her dry lips and cast a longing glance at the tall Georgian windows which gave the impression of having been hermetically sealed since the day they were installed. Then she transferred her gaze to her hands, clasped tensely together in her lap. They were nice-looking hands, she thought judiciously. A little too slender perhaps, but perfectly capable as she had proved over and over again during the past two years. And very bare.

Her lips tightened slightly as almost involuntarily her right hand moved protectively to conceal her left. Surely by this time she should have forgotten what it had been like to wear, briefly, that broad band of antique gold, just as she had tried to forget the emotions she had experienced when it had been placed on her finger.

And in that at least she had succeeded, she thought. Wasn't that precisely why she was here today?

Mr Bristow was still on the telephone, his voice reassuring, his head nodding firmly as he pressed each point home. They'd hardly had time to do more than exchange a conventional greeting before the call came through, so she had no idea what news he had for her. She stared at the buff folders tied with tape littering the polished top of his desk. One of them she supposed concerned her, but she had no idea which it was. She tried unobtrusively to crane her neck and read some of the names and references printed on the folders, but it was obvious that Mr Bristow was briskly winding up the call, so she leaned back in the comfortable leather chair and tried to give an impression of relaxation.

'Sorry about that,' he said as he replaced the receiver. 'Slight case of panic, I'm afraid.'

'And you're looking at another.' She tried a laugh, but it wasn't a great success.

Mr Bristow's eyes studied her keenly for a moment, then he reached for one of the files. It was a very thin one, she noticed, containing only a few papers.

She tried again. 'I—I hope you have good news for me?'

Mr Bristow pursed his lips. 'I'm afraid not, or more truthfully, I have no news at all. Your—er—Mr Lloyd has simply not answered any of my letters.'

'I see.' Davina bit her lip. 'Well, perhaps he hasn't received them. If he's still moving around all the time . . .'

Mr Bristow shook his head. 'When there was no response to the first letter, I sent the remainder by recorded delivery,' he said. 'And Mr Lloyd is certainly not—moving around at present. He's been back in Britain for some considerable time, or so we discovered when we traced him.'

'Back in Britain?' Davina echoed bewilderedly. 'But when? There's been nothing in the papers about it.'

'Perhaps he wanted it that way,' Mr Bristow suggested. He gave the papers in front of him a frowning look. 'I can assure you that our information is quite correct. He's resident at present at'—his frown deepened—'Plas Gwyn, Moel y Ddraig. I'm not at all sure my pronunciation is correct, but . . .'

'I get the general idea,' Davina said with a touch of impatience. She was secretly appalled, and her mind was whirling madly. She had accustomed herself for so long to the idea that Gethyn was at a safe distance on the other side of the Atlantic that the news that he had returned quietly, without the blaze of publicity which had attended the majority of his comings and goings in the past, was a severe shock.

At least she could be thankful that he was not actually here in London, she told herself.

She swallowed, forcing herself to speak calmly. 'So he's

back in Wales. Well, that should make things—easier, surely?'

'Not if he refuses to reply to our letters,' Mr Bristow pointed out. 'Can you think of any explanation for his continuing silence? When you first consulted me, you gave me the strongest impression that your—Mr Lloyd would be only too glad to consent to a divorce.'

Davina's hands were gripped together so tightly that her knuckles showed white. She said evenly, 'That was what I had every reason to believe. My—my husband's—exploits during our separation have been well-enough documented.' The colour rose faintly in her cheeks. 'I can't imagine a single reason why he should wish to prolong this—farce a day longer than necessary.'

Mr Bristow sighed. 'As I pointed out to you before, newspaper gossip in itself does not constitute acceptable evidence. And you realise of course that if your husband does not give his written consent to the divorce you would have to wait a further three years for your freedom.'

'But that's monstrous!' Davina was indignant.

'It's the law,' Mr Bristow reminded her placidly. He hesitated for a moment. 'I can always write again, pressing Mr Lloyd for a reply, but I was wondering . . . Have you—er—Miss Greer—considered the personal approach?'

'Are you suggesting that I should go to Gethyn and—ask him to agree to a divorce?'

'It has been done before,' Mr Bristow said drily. 'It could result in a perfectly amicable arrangement, particularly as there are only the two of you concerned. Sometimes where there are children to be considered, difficulties can arise, but that isn't the case here.'

'No,' Davina said woodenly. 'That—isn't the case. But I was hoping to avoid having to see my husband again.'

'I think some kind of interview is almost inevitable,' Mr Bristow said kindly. 'For one thing, we have to convince the court that a real attempt has been made at reconciliation.'

Davina's face burned hotly. 'That's totally impossible.'

'Perhaps, but you must at least go through the motions, Miss Greer. It's not sufficient, I'm afraid, merely to remove your wedding ring and revert to your maiden name. The divorce laws may have eased in recent years, but they are not yet that lax,' he remarked with something like asperity. 'Perhaps you would care to think over what I have said and then let me have your further instructions in a day or two.'

'Yes,' Davina gave him a constrained smile as she rose to her feet. 'Maybe that would be best.'

'I'm sure it would.' Mr Bristow came round the desk to shake hands cordially with her at the door. 'Divorce is a messy business, Miss Greer, at the best of times. If there is a chance of reducing the unpleasantness to any extent, then I think you should take it.'

Davina's thoughts were in total confusion as she emerged from the offices to the warmth of the summer afternoon outside. Officially, she had the rest of the afternoon off, and she supposed she should go home where her mother would be eager to hear what had happened. But she would be expecting to hear that Gethyn had agreed to the divorce and that a date had already been set for the hearing, Davina thought wryly. What had actually transpired would be much less acceptable. Besides, this was one of her mother's bridge afternoons, and Davina had no wish for her private affairs to feature over the tea-cups once the game was over.

She paused irresolutely on the crowded pavement, then hailed a passing taxi, telling the driver to take her to the Park. At least she would be delaying the inevitable recriminations for a while. Also the stuffy atmosphere in Mr Bristow's room seemed to have given her a slight headache and she wanted to be able to think clearly.

She had been completely taken aback by Mr Bristow's suggestion that she should seek Gethyn out and ask him to allow the divorce to go ahead. He had made it all sound so civilised and reasonable, she thought blankly, but then he had not had to suffer those few brief weeks of her marriage to Gethyn.

People said, didn't they, that to marry in haste was to repent at leisure. Well, she could vouch for the truth of that. Her marriage had been the wild, extravagant impulse of an hour and almost as soon regretted. And now her two years of repentance were drawing to an end and she could be free again—but only if Gethyn agreed. This was what stuck in her throat—this dependence on the whim of a man she had not even seen for two years. That, and the knowledge that he was probably maintaining this silence deliberately to annoy and worry her. There could be no other reason. He had no more wish to continue this nominal relationship than she had.

She paid off the driver and walked slowly into the Park. There were people everywhere and the sun shone down out of a cloudless sky, but Davina felt cold and alone.

Perhaps this hadn't been such a good idea after all, she thought, skirting a pair of lovers entwined on the grass and oblivious of everything but each other. Once—a long time ago—she and Gethyn had lain like that in this very park and let the world walk indulgently past them. She bit her lip, remembering how he had overcome her reluctance, her protests, drawing her down beside him with compelling hands, his eyes narrowed against the sun laughing up at her, reducing her scruples to absurdity.

Then his mouth had found hers and she was lost, caught in a web of delight from which not even the thought of her mother's shocked disapproval of such conduct could release her. His lips had explored her face, her throat and shoulders, rousing her nerve-endings to rapturous life. She had been amazed by the ardour of her own response, scared by the feelings his lightest touch could evoke. It had been Gethyn who had moved away first, she recalled painfully, levering himself away from her and sitting for a moment, his head buried in his hands. Then he had looked up and seen her, watching him anxiously, her face flushed, her eyes enormous, her mouth blurred and swollen a little from his passion, and the harshness of his dark face had softened momentarily.

'Come on.' He got lithely to his feet. 'Let's get out of here before we get arrested.'

The following day, over lunch, he had abruptly asked her to marry him. And she, bewitched by his lovemaking into a

frank longing to belong to him completely, had eagerly
agreed. It was only later—a long time later—that it occurred to her that he had never said he loved her.

Davina quickened her steps, instinctively fighting the
torment that she had released upon herself with these
memories. What a child she had been, she lashed herself
derisively. No doubt Gethyn had supposed that at nineteen
she shared the slick, knowing sophistication of most of her
contemporaries. Her eager innocence must have come as an
unwelcome surprise to him.

Her mother's opposition to the marriage had been instant and hostile.

'You can't marry him,' Mrs Greer said, her face white and
pinched. 'A man like that! He must be twice your age, and
he's positively uncouth.'

'He's a writer—a poet.' Davina had tried to reason with
her. 'I know he doesn't correspond with your idea of one—
but he's famous already ...'

'On the strength of two novels and a few poems,' her
mother had sneered. 'A television celebrity—until the next
nine-day wonder comes along, and then he'll soon be forgotten about.'

'Uncle Philip doesn't think so.'

'Of course your uncle would defend him.' Mrs Greer
smiled thinly. 'He's his publisher, after all. Oh God, I wish
you'd never gone to that party, then you would never have
met him.'

'Oh, but I would.' Davina lifted her head, her eyes shining. 'It was fate.'

'Fate!' her mother scoffed angrily, and turned away.
'Well, you won't marry with my consent, Davina.'

'Then we'll marry without it,' Davina said angrily, and
saw her mother flinch. Compunction overcame her then,
and she went to her, laying a hand on her arm. 'Mother, if
you would just get to know Gethyn—properly.'

'As you do, I suppose,' Mrs Greer returned impatiently.
'How long has this—whirlwind courtship lasted? Three
weeks? Do you really imagine that's a sufficient period of
time to find out about a man with whom you intend to

spend the rest of your life? If you must continue with this
—relationship, why not just become engaged? At least one
can withdraw from an engagement honourably before too
much harm is done—but marriage!' Mrs Greer shuddered.

'I don't want to withdraw from it,' Davina said desperately. 'And neither does Gethyn.'

Her mother's lip curled. 'That I can well understand.
He's doing very well for himself, after all. A miner's son
from some obscure pit village in Wales, marrying his publisher's niece. Another rung on the ladder from rags to
riches. Of course he wants to go through with it. He'd be a
fool not to. No doubt by now someone will have told him
about the money that's to come to you from your father's
estate when you're twenty-five, and that will be an added
incentive.'

There was a long silence, and then Davina said huskily,
'That—that's an appalling thing to say.'

'The truth often does hurt,' he mother returned inimic-
ally.

Mrs Greer had not attended the ceremony at Caxton Hall
a few days later. Uncle Philip had been there, however,
with Gethyn's agent Alec Marks to act as the other witness.
It had been swift and rather impersonal and very far from
the sort of wedding she had once day-dreamed about when
she was younger. Gethyn was different too in a dark formal suit which contrasted strangely with the denims and
dark roll-collared sweaters she was accustomed to seeing
him wear.

That was what he had been wearing the first time she
saw him at the party Uncle Philip had given to launch his
new volume of poetry. Poems were often considered by
publishers to be a drug on the market, and yet this book
would sell, her uncle knew, because Gethyn Lloyd had written it.

The first thing Davina had thought when she set eyes on
him was that he didn't look at all like the star of the show.
She had been at many such parties in the past, and writers
often, she found, behaved either with a becoming diffidence
or an excessive eagerness to please when confronted by the

media men, or sometimes both. Not so Gethyn Lloyd.

He hadn't been the tallest man in the room, yet he had
seemed so. There was something about his lean, muscular
body, the dark harsh lines of his face, that made the other
men seem positively effete. He stood a little apart, gazing
broodingly into the glass he held, his dark brows drawn
frowningly together above that hawk's beak of a nose
which surely must have been broken at some stage in his
career. Then he had looked up suddenly, so suddenly that
she had been unable to avert her gaze in time, and his cool
green eyes had locked startlingly with hers. And the firm
sensual lines of his mouth had relaxed into a smile—not
the hurtful mockery she had come so painfully to know
later—but with a charm that made her heart turn over.

He came to her side, dealing summarily with a woman
journalist from a popular daily who tried to detain him. His
eyes swept over her, missing nothing, she thought dazedly,
from the dark auburn hair piled smoothly on top of her
shapely head to the silver buckles on the shoes just visible
beneath the deep plum velvet trousers.

'I don't know who you are, but I'd like to take you to
dinner tonight.' His voice was low and resonant, with an
underlying lilt which was undeniably attractive.

She smiled. 'Perhaps you'll change your mind when you
learn my identity,' she said lightly. 'I'm Davina Greer.'

He studied her reflectively for a moment, then swung to
look at Philip Greer, deep in conversation at the opposite
end of the room. 'Daughter? You're not much alike.'

'Niece—and I'm supposed to resemble my mother's side
of the family.'

'Hm.' That devastating green glance was on her again,
assessing the candour of her hazel eyes under their long
sweep of lashes, the high delicacy of her cheekbones and
the sweet vulnerable curve of her mouth. 'Then I must meet
her. They say, don't they, that if you want to know what
your girl will look like in years to come, take a look at her
mother.'

'Do they?' She lifted her brows coolly, trying to conceal
the instinctive tremor that had gone through her when he'd

said 'your girl'. 'I've never heard that before.'

'Oh, I've a fund of such information,' he said softly. 'Stick with me, lovely, and you could learn a lot.'

She was on her guard instantly, aware that there was an implication in his words that put them squarely into the category of doubtful remarks, to be dealt with by cool politeness. She gave him a formal smile, and changed the subject.

'Will you be in London long, Mr Lloyd?'

'Long enough.' His eyes never left her face. 'And at least until I've persuaded you to have dinner with me.'

'You're very persistent,' she said helplessly.

'I've been accused of worse things,' he returned laconically. He put out a finger and lifted her chin slightly, forcing her to look at him. 'What's the matter? Surely I can't be the first man who's fancied you?'

No, she thought, but you're the first man I've ever—fancied, and I don't know what to do. I'm frightened.

She smiled again, moved slightly so that his hand was no longer even fractionally against her skin. 'Well, hardly.'

'So what's the problem, lovely?'

She managed to meet his gaze. 'Nothing, I suppose. Thank you, Mr Lloyd. I'd like to have dinner with you.'

Which was a tame way to describe this sweet insidious excitement which was beginning to take possession of her.

'Good.' He drained the contents of his glass. 'Shall we go?'

She stared at him. 'But the party—it isn't over yet.'

'It is as far as I'm concerned. I've answered all their questions. Now I'm leaving them in peace to drink and talk at each other, and that's what they really want to do. Most of them only came here today anyway because someone in the higher echelons suddenly decided that poetry might be trendy. Besides, there's always a story in me—a miner's son who can actually string words together like a real person.'

'That's rather bitter, isn't it?'

'Probably, but it's the way I'm feeling at the moment. In-depth interviews and expensive whisky seem to affect me like that. I'm relying on you to exorcise all my evil spirits.'

'That sounds a tall order on such a short acquaintance.'
She pulled a wry face.

'Who said our acquaintance was going to be short?' he
said. 'And you don't have to worry. I think, if you wanted,
you could coax wild beasts and dragons to eat out of your
hand if you put your mind to it.'

She was embarrassed at the personal turn to the conversation and took refuge in flippancy. 'Even a Welsh
dragon?'

He gave her a long look, and she made herself meet it
steadily.

'Oh, that most of all, girl,' he said. 'That most of all.'

Somehow she found herself apologising to Uncle Philip
for her early departure and calling goodbyes to the surprised glances which were noting it around the room.

As they waited for the lift in the corridor, she began to
laugh.

'It's far too early for dinner. There won't be a restaurant
open.'

'Then we'll walk and talk and generally further our short
acquaintance.' He allowed her to precede him into the lift.
The doors closed noiselessly, shutting them into a tight
enclosed world where they were quite alone.

Davina said breathlessly, 'We need the ground floor. You
have to press the button.'

He slanted a glance at her. 'I've been in lifts before. Why
are you so nervous?'

She moistened her lips. 'I'm not.'

'Don't lie to me, Davina. Not now, not ever. What do you
imagine I'm going to do? Leap on you?'

She felt herself go crimson. 'Of course not,' she denied
too quickly.

His lips twisted slightly. 'Then you're far too trusting,' he
told her mockingly, and sent the lift on its way to street
level.

She was recalled abruptly back to the present as a child's
coloured ball bounced towards her and she instinctively put
out a foot to stop it. She stood quite still for a moment,

assimilating her surroundings, and telling herself that these things were all in the past now and could only have the power to hurt her if she allowed them to. But her eyes were stinging suddenly and she fumbled in her handbag for her dark glasses, insisting to herself that it was only the sunlight that was too strong.

She was dazzled now, as she'd been dazzled then, and as she walked on, the words, 'Too trusting. Too trusting . . .' began to sound a bitter knell in her tired brain.

In the end, she took another taxi and went back to the office. The publishing firm of Hanson Greer was situated in a quiet street not far from the Post Office Tower. She pushed open the glass door and went in with a smile for the receptionist in her panelled cubicle. She accepted a list of the people who had telephoned her during her absence and took the lift up to her office.

Her mother had not wanted her to work here, yet at the time it had seemed a perfectly logical thing to do. Her father had been a director of the firm until his death, and if she had been a boy, it would have been quite natural for her to follow him into publishing. And this was supposed to be the age of equal opportunities, so . . . Besides, Uncle Philip's offer of a job had come just when she needed it most—when she was looking round desperately for something to fill this emotional vacuum inside herself, and she had seized it with relief.

She knew the reason for her mother's opposition, of course. She was terrified that Davina would be brought into contact with Gethyn again through her work. But it hadn't happened. For one thing, as far as she had known until today Gethyn was still in America, teaching creative writing at some New England college. And for another, in the two years they had been apart, he had apparently not produced another manuscript of his own. While he had been in the States, he had written the screenplay for the successful film of his first book, *A Power for Good*, but no new work had been forthcoming from him, and although he had never discussed it with her, Davina knew this had been a major disappointment for her uncle.

She went into her small room and sat down with a sigh, her eyes fixed absently on the scrap of paper in her hand. She really ought to make a start on returning these calls. One of them at least would probably be urgent. But the names and numbers kept dancing meaninglessly in front of her eyes, and eventually she dropped the piece of paper impatiently into her in-tray to await her attention in the morning.

Her door opened and the smooth fair head of Jan Preston, her uncle's secretary, appeared.

'Oh, you are back,' she exclaimed in surprise. 'I've been trying to get you at home. Mr Greer would like a word with you.'

Davina groaned inwardly. For a moment she toyed with the idea of asking Jan to forget she had seen her while she made her escape, but she soon abandoned it. Jan was a pleasant woman, but she was simply not on those kind of terms with her. So instead she smiled and murmured her thanks, promising she would be along presently.

When Jan vanished, she got up and walked the few paces to the window. There was little to see but a patch of sky framed by other people's roofs, and the odd pigeon or two, but when she had first come there, she had spent a lot of time staring out at that limited view until she felt she knew every slate and every Victorian chimneypot.

Her fingers drummed restlessly on the white-painted sill. She knew why Uncle Philip wanted to see her, of course. He knew precisely where she had been that afternoon, and could presumably restrain his curiosity no longer.

She supposed she could not blame him under the circumstances. After all, the other party involved was one of his protegés, a writer for whom he had confidently predicted great things. And he had been right. Both Gethyn's novels had been runaway best-sellers, here and in the States, and he promised to become a major force in the poetic world as well. Since then—two years of silence.

Her uncle's voice sounded preoccupied as he called out

'Come in' in reply to her brief tap on the door. He was dictating some letters into a dictaphone as she entered and he signalled to her to take a seat while he went on talking '. . . and shall look forward to seeing you on the 21st. Yours.' He switched off the machine and smiled at her.

'Hello, my dear. How did it go? Did this tame lawyer your mother found produce the goods?'

'Well,' Davina considered her polished fingernails, 'at least he's produced Gethyn. He's back in Wales. Did you know?'

'No.' Was it her imagination, or had there been a slight pause before the monosyllable? Davina glanced up quickly, but Philip Greer was leaning back in his chair, his frowning gaze fixed musingly on a ballpoint pen he was twirling in his fingers. 'But all the same I'm pleased to hear it.'

'Why?'

'Because it might just mean he's ready to settle down and get some work done—some real work.'

Davina bent her head. 'I see.'

Philip Greer gazed at her rather ironically. 'What did you expect me to say? I haven't any other hopes where Gethyn's concerned any more. I'm resigned to the fact that you're determined to put an end to this marriage of yours.'

She looked up indignantly. 'Well, what do you expect?' she demanded in turn. 'This marriage of mine, as you put it, hasn't existed for two years. It barely existed before then.' She gave a bitter laugh. 'If I'd ignored my upbringing and simply gone to bed with Gethyn, it need never have taken place at all. Now there's an irony for you!'

Philip Greer made an abrupt movement. 'If you're saying that the basis for your marriage was no more than physical attraction, then I should point out that a great many successful unions have started out on little else.'

'I see,' she said again. 'Perhaps I pitched my own expectations too high.'

He sighed. 'Now I've made you angry, my dear, and I didn't intend that. I've always felt—responsible in some ways for what happened between you and Gethyn, and I know your mother shares my viewpoint,' he added wryly.

She flushed. 'I know. I've tried to tell her . . .'

'My dear, no one will ever convince Vanessa about anything she doesn't wish to hear. And I'm afraid she "took
agin" Gethyn the first time she saw him. And he didn't
help, of course. He needn't have made it quite so clear that
he was indifferent to her and her opinion of him. If he'd
just pretended . . .'

She gave a strained smile. 'Pretence was beyond him, I'm
afraid. He—he couldn't even pretend with me—pretend
that I mattered, or that he cared, even a little.'

'Are you so sure he didn't?'

'Uncle Philip,' Davina stared at him, 'how can you ask
that? You know what happened. He was in the States and I
was here—in hospital, losing his baby. I sent for him—I
begged him to come back and be with me. But he was far
too busy with some television chat show. He just didn't
want to know. Every time the door opened in that hospital
room, I thought it was going to be him. Only it never was.
And even then, I swallowed my pride when it was all over
and telephoned him. Do you know the answer I got? He
was resting and couldn't be disturbed. Later that night I
wrote to him and told him I was leaving him. He never replied to my letter either, and I've never heard from him
from that day to this.' She forced a smile. 'I'm sorry about
the downbeat ending, but . . .'

'Don't be flip, my dear. It's unsuitable in this context.'
Her uncle was silent for a while. 'I can only say that I find
his—lack of response totally incredible. I can't help wondering if it would have made any difference if you had gone
to see him, instead of writing. Letters can go astray, you
know. Phone messages may not always be passed on, and
sometimes are distorted in the re-telling. Did it ever occur
to you that there might have been some—misunderstanding?'

'One, perhaps. Not three,' she said quietly. 'And I feel
sure his silence was—is—deliberate. He won't answer my
solicitor's letters either.'

Philip Greer raised his eyebrows. 'Indeed? So what's the
next move?'

'I'm not altogether sure.' She hesitated. 'Mr Bristow has suggested that I should do—what you've just said—go and see Gethyn and try and talk him into agreeing to a divorce.'

'And you said?'

'I didn't know what to say. Frankly, I was stunned.'

'But you didn't reject the idea out of hand?'

'No.' Davina paused bleakly. 'I wouldn't reject any idea that might help me to be free of him.'

'Hm.' Her uncle gave her a narrow look. 'Well, if you do decide to seek him out, I wouldn't be quite so frank. In fact, it's a pity that the divorce has to be your sole motive for going to Wales. Now I wonder . . .' he relapsed into frowning silence. Then he glanced at her. 'How would it be if this was ostensibly a business trip? After all, Gethyn is still under contract to us, and we need another book from him. Go and see him—but as my representative, not as his estranged wife. Don't even mention Bristow's letters or the divorce, unless he does.'

Davina shook her head. 'He wouldn't be taken in by that.'

'I'm not saying he would be, but at least he wouldn't be expecting it. I also know Gethyn, my dear, and I'm sure an oblique approach would work best. It's a pity we didn't think of it before your mother involved Bristow, but it's too late to do anything about that now. What I'm trying to say is that you won't get what you want by flying off to Wales and quarrelling with Gethyn. That would only harden his attitude, and that's the last thing you want to do.'

'Yes.' Davina was silent for a moment. 'I suppose it's worth a try. At least it's better than doing nothing—than just waiting for Gethyn to make the first move.'

Philip Greer tapped his upper lip thoughtfully with his forefinger. 'Tell him too that there could be another tour in the offing. Oh, it's quite true,' he added hastily, meeting Davina's quizzical look. 'There have been a number of overtures in the past few months. I've just been waiting for the psychological moment to put it to Gethyn. I had to sell the last one to him, as a matter of fact, but you probably know that.'

Yes, Davina thought, as she walked slowly back to her own office. She had known that. But not until afterwards—after she had agreed to marry Gethyn. And then it had been altogether different because the trip to America was going to be their honeymoon—not the handful of nights in the suite of a luxury hotel which Uncle Philip was giving them as a wedding present. She had been as excited as a child at Christmas at the prospect, thrilled to the core as well because Gethyn had told her that if she hadn't wanted to go with him, he would have called the whole thing off. It gave her a wonderful feeling of power, a feeling of being necessary. It had been a delusion, of course, as she quickly found out, but for that brief time she had never been happier. She had dreamed of the places they would see together—New York, San Francisco, even New Orleans.

'And Niagara Falls,' Gethyn had said, grinning. 'Isn't that where all self-respecting honeymooners go?'

Only by the time he had left for the States—alone—the honeymoon was already over.

Davina closed her door behind her, and sank down in the chair behind her desk, reaching automatically for the manuscript on top of the pile in front of her. She began to read it, forcing herself relentlessly to concentrate, but it was useless. It was the story of a failed marriage, and even in the first chapter there were words, phrases, scraps of dialogue which struck a painful chord in her own memory. At last she pushed it almost desperately to one side and buried her head in her folded arms on the desktop.

When had it all started to go wrong? she asked herself. Hadn't her mother sown the first seeds of doubt, even before the wedding ceremony had taken place? She had come into Davina's room on the morning of the wedding and watched her as she packed a suitcase.

Davina had just been smoothing the folds of a filmy drift of nightgown when she had caught sight of her mother's expression in the dressing-table mirror, her eyes hooded, her lips thin with distaste.

'Mother,' she had said, gently enough, 'please try to be happy for me.'

'Happy?' Her mother's laugh had been almost shrill. 'Happy that you're rushing headlong into marriage with a complete stranger? You may think you know all you need to know, but you're a child. What do you know of men—of what living with a man means? I was fortunate. Your father was a kind man—considerate, undemanding. But *he* won't be like that. You'd better enjoy your innocence while you can. It won't be yours much longer. Wait until you've been alone with him, tonight, and then talk to me about happiness!'

She had turned then and gone from the room, leaving Davina staring after her with startled eyes and parted lips. She had resumed her packing, but the golden glow which surrounded her had dissipated somewhat. It was the nearest her mother had come, or ever would come, she realised, to discussing the sexual relationship with her. She had always sensed instinctively that her parents' marriage had been lacking in certain aspects. Widowhood, she had often thought wryly, suited her mother far better than being a wife had done. But this was the first time Mrs Greer had ever spoken openly on the subject, and made her disgust plain.

And later when she arrived at Caxton Hall and saw Gethyn waiting for her, tall and unfamiliar in his dark suit, her mother's words had returned to her mind with paralysing force, freezing the smile on her lips. Even while the registrar was marrying them, she could feel Gethyn's eyes on her, questioningly. Afterwards Uncle Philip had taken them to the Ritz and they had drunk champagne, and she had found herself acting the part of the radiant bride, laughing that little bit too much, smiling until her mouth ached. And all the time knowing that he was watching her, and not wanting to meet his eyes in case she read in them a message she wasn't ready for yet. But she had to be ready, that was the whole point. She was his wife now and very soon now they would be alone and he would take her in his arms and everything would be all right. She held on to that thought with quiet desperation. She was just being stupid —bridal nerves. That was all it was—it had to be.

After all, in the past weeks there had been times when

she had clung to Gethyn, glorying in his desire for her, but armoured at the same time, she realised, by the iron self-control he seemed to be able to exercise where she was concerned. Now there was no longer any need for that control. She belonged to him.

She sat beside him in the taxi as they drove to the small flat he was renting to fetch his own case, not touching him and thankful for the taxi-driver's cheerful presence. She would liked to have made an excuse and waited for him in the cab, but he made it quite clear he expected her to accompany him up to the flat. She stood silently while he unlocked the door and then walked ahead of him into the small living room. This was all strange too, she thought, even though it was where they would be living when they returned from the hotel until they left again for the U.S.A. She wandered round the room while Gethyn collected some things from the bedroom. It was difficult to imagine herself sitting in either of the fireside chairs reading while Gethyn worked at the table behind her. She peered into the kitchenette where she would soon be cooking the meals and a feeling of total inadequacy began to invade her.

It was as if some romantic veil had been suddenly torn from her eyes and she was seeing life as it really was for the first time. Where had they gone—all those hours she had spent with Gethyn, wandering round art galleries, browsing through bookshops? He had taken her to dinner, to the theatre, walked with her along the Embankment and through the parks. Sometimes he had kissed her, and she put a hand almost fearfully against her lips. It wasn't a great deal on which to base a relationship as intimate as marriage, yet this was what she had done. What did she know about him really—except where he had been to school and university and the titles of the books he had written? She knew his parents were dead and that he was an only child like herself, and preferred Italian food to Chinese. She shook her head almost dazedly.

She heard a board creak behind her and turned to find him leaning against the bedroom door jamb watching her. He had discarded his jacket and loosened his tie and looked completely at home, which she supposed he was. She was the stranger here. The little fish, suddenly and disastrously out of water.

'Come here.' His tone was gentle enough, but there was an underlying note of command, of ownership even, which made her mouth dry.

She tried to smile. 'The taxi will be waiting.'

His brows rose lazily. 'I sent the taxi away. We can call another when we're ready. Now, come here.'

Her reluctance must have been obvious for by the time her lagging steps had got her across the room to him, he had straightened with a jerk and was frowning.

'It's a little soon for second thoughts, isn't it?' he asked sarcastically, and she flushed.

'I—I don't know what you mean.'

'Of course you know,' he jibed. 'Any resemblance between you and the loving girl I kissed last night is purely coincidental. My God, I don't think you've touched me voluntarily all day.' He took her by the shoulders, his eyes searching hers. 'What the hell's the matter with you?'

'Nothing,' she lied. 'It's all been a bit of a strain, that's all. And Mummy was being—difficult this morning.'

Gethyn murmured something under his breath that she prudently failed to hear. Then his grip had tightened, compelling her towards him.

'Hello, wife,' he said quietly, and bent and kissed her on the mouth. She made herself remain passive under his touch, waiting for that familiar warm tide of feeling to engulf her, but there was nothing. It was as if her warm flesh and blood had been transformed to marble. She was incapable of even the slightest response, and presently he released her. She had closed her eyes involuntarily as he had bent towards her, and she kept them closed, afraid to encounter his anger, until she knew that he had moved away.

When she ventured to open them, she found he had returned to the bedroom and was focussing all his attention on fastening the straps round his case. She bit her lip.

'Shall I make some coffee?' She strove for normality.

'If you want some,' he said, his voice expressionless. 'Can you find everything?'

'Well, I shall have to learn some time,' she returned without thinking, and blushed stormily as his sardonic gaze met hers.

'That's true,' he observed smoothly, and swung the case from the bed to the floor. She turned away hastily and went to the kitchenette. She filled the kettle and plugged it in, and found the remains of a pint of milk in the refrigerator.

She was searching through the cupboards for the jar of coffee when Gethyn came in. Immediately the admittedly cramped area of the kitchen seemed to shrink to the proportions of a postage stamp.

'Look,' she pointed to the milk. 'That wants using up.'

'Perhaps.' He came to the cupboard and leaned down, his arm brushing hers. It was as much as she could do not to flinch. He produced the coffee jar and set it down on the narrow worktop. 'Unless we decide to stay.'

'To stay?' She could hear the nervousness in her own voice, and knew it would not be lost on him either. 'But we're going to the hotel.'

'I'm not so sure that's such a good idea.' His face was enigmatic as he spooned coffee into the waiting beakers. 'This is going to be our home, at least on a temporary basis. I don't see why we shouldn't move straight in, and forgo your uncle's offer, kind though it was.'

'Oh, but we couldn't!' The kettle was boiling and she moved hurriedly to swith it off.

'Why not?' He leaned one elbow on the worktop, watching her levelly. 'Careful of that kettle. You're going to scald yourself.'

She set it down, her heart thumping. 'Because—because it would hurt Uncle Phil's feelings. It's his wedding present to us and . . .'

'I could phone him and explain the situation. I'm sure he would understand.'

'Well, that's more than I do.' She lifted the kettle and filled the beakers.

'I simply get the feeling that the implications of the

bridal suite are proving a little too much for you at the moment,' he said unemotionally. 'I'll ask him just to postpone it for a few months, if you like, until you're in a mood to appreciate it more.'

She was panic-stricken. The flat was so small. What possibility of privacy did it afford? She added a splash of milk to her coffee and sipped at it almost distractedly. She preferred it with sugar, but she did not wish Gethyn to join her on another search for the commodity. She thought fast.

'I think it's too late to change our minds now,' she said rapidly. 'The hotel will be expecting us. Besides, I didn't really expect to have to do housework on my honeymoon.'

It should have sounded coquettish, but it came out as petulance, and she wished it unsaid. Gethyn's dark face was still and enigmatic.

He said coolly, 'As you wish, then,' and drank his coffee with a slight grimace.

While he phoned for a taxi to take them to the hotel, Davina rinsed the beakers under the tap. She caught a glimpse of her reflection in the kitchen window, her eyes much wider and brighter than usual, but that could be the champagne, and a tiny flush of colour high on her cheekbones. She looked as if she was running a temperature, yet inside she felt deathly cold.

She was still cold when the hotel porter ushered them into the suite. Everything was there waiting for them—more champagne on ice, red roses—lovers' flowers, filling the air with their scent, baskets of fruit. She glanced round and saw through the half-open door the gleam of a gold satin bedspread, and hurriedly averted her gaze. Gethyn was tipping the man, who was asking, after an appreciative word of thanks, if they wished to have dinner in the suite rather than downstairs in the restaurant.

'We'll dine up here,' Gethyn said. 'We can order later, I suppose.'

'Of course, sir.' The man's voice was deferential, eager to please.

'Oh no,' Davina broke in, aghast. 'I—I mean—wouldn't it be more fun to have dinner downstairs ...' Her voice tailed away uncomfortably. She knew that they were both looking at her, the porter with a kind of sly amusement under his deferential manner, and Gethyn with an anger that held no deference at all. He turned to the porter.

'My wife prefers the restaurant. Perhaps you would make the necessary arrangements.'

When the door closed behind the man, he said softly and chillingly, 'Do you think you could manage to conceal this aversion you have for being alone with me in front of the hotel staff?'

He strode across the sitting room to a door on the opposite side and opened it, glancing in. He was smiling when he turned, but his eyes were like green ice.

'The instinct that brought you here was quite right, lovely. Every modern convenience at your disposal—even a second bedroom for the bestowal of an importunate bridegroom.' He stared round the luxurious sitting room. 'And what shall we call this, eh? No Man's Land, perhaps? Shall I wait for you here when it gets to dinner time, or would you prefer to eat separately too?'

She said, and there was a sob under her breath, 'Gethyn?' She was asking for his tenderness, his understanding, but he had gone and the door was shut behind him. She was alone and afraid.

With a long shuddering sigh, Davina sat up at her desk and pushed her hair back wearily from her pale face. She was still alone, she thought. But at least she was no longer afraid, and to prove it she would go to this place in Wales and meet Gethyn face to face once again.

CHAPTER TWO

THE signpost for Moel y Ddraig had said four miles, but Davina seemed to have been driving for hours and there was still no sign of any habitation. The narrow road wound determinedly on ahead of her, leading her deeper and deeper into the very heart of the valley.

She had encountered little other traffic, so she had been able to pay some heed to the beauty around her. It was wild and rugged when compared to some of the rounded green hills she had seen that day, with harsh, rocky outcrops thrusting through the short green turf and clumps of purple heather. There seemed to be sheep grazing everywhere, like tiny tufts of cotton wool against the vivid landscape. The sky was a deep tranquil blue with only the faintest tracery of high white cloud.

If only this had been the start of a holiday, Davina thought ruefully, she might have imagined herself in heaven. As it was, not even the wild charm of the valley could rid her of the insidious feeling of dread that was beginning to pervade her consciousness. She was already regretting quite bitterly that she had ever set out on this strange journey.

But she wouldn't turn round and go back. Now she was here, she would go through with it. In her briefcase was a letter from Uncle Philip, setting out details of the proposed American tour—her credentials for being here. Not that she expected Gethyn to be taken in by that for one minute. It was merely a face-saver and she knew it, but at least her presence here in Wales would mean that she could test his feelings about divorce.

She had tried quite vainly to explain this to her mother. Mrs Greer had been stunned into silence when Davina had awkwardly broken the news of her proposed trip and its dual purpose. Then, and more disturbingly, she had burst into tears.

'You're going back to him,' she had repeated over and over again. 'In spite of everything that's happened, you're going back to him.'

'No.' Davina had attempted to reason with her. 'I'm going solely to find out, if I can, why he has ignored Mr Bristow's letters. And I have some papers from Uncle Philip to deliver as well.'

'Oh, yes, Philip!' Her mother had rounded on her, her eyes flashing. 'Naturally, he's involved. He'd be glad to see you reconciled to that—creature, if only to spite me. He's never liked me.'

Davina felt suddenly very weary. 'If Uncle Philip really felt like that, I doubt whether he'd go to these lengths to show it,' she said. 'This tour that's being laid on is quite genuine.'

Mrs Greer produced a lace-trimmed handkerchief and sat twisting it in her hands. Her eyes when she looked at Davina were brooding and full of resentment.

'I still see no need for you to go,' she said. 'If it's all that important, Philip could go himself—or send someone else.'

'He is sending someone else,' Davina insisted gently. 'He's sending me. I do work for Hanson Greer, you know. Please try to understand, Mother. The easiest way for me to get a divorce is to persuade Gethyn to agree to it. If he won't answer letters then it will have to be in person. I just want us to end our marriage in a civilised manner . . .'

'Civilised!' her mother cut in, with a bitter laugh. 'With that barbarian? He has no decent feelings—leaving you ill and alone while he gallivanted across the United States.'

'I wasn't ill when he went,' Davina pointed out. 'In fact it was you. You had that bad dose of 'flu, and I stayed to look after you.'

'Oh, I see.' Her mother's lips were trembling again. 'So it's all my fault. But for my inconvenient virus, you'd have gone trailing after him like some pet dog.'

Davina bit her lip. 'I don't know what I would have

done,' she said. 'And there's little point in discussing it now. I—didn't go.'

Looking back, she realised it was not merely the nursing of her mother, who had been a fractious patient, that had made her so tired, but the early pregnancy she had only dimly begun to suspect. Mrs Greer had refused to have a private nurse, and had insisted on Davina doing everything for her during her illness and convalescence, and it had been while Davina was helping her mother downstairs one day that she herself had slipped and fallen and precipitated the loss of her baby.

Afterwards she had wondered sometimes if she had confided her suspicion that she might be pregnant to Gethyn whether it would have made any difference, but on the whole she doubted it. Gethyn had already chosen his own path, and his hasty marriage had only been a temporary aberration from this. His solitary departure for the States had been an acknowledgment of their mistake, and a repudiation of his part in it.

Perhaps, Davina thought painfully, it was just as well he had not responded to her urgent call for him when she was in hospital. They might have been together even now, tied only by her dependence and his pity. It was a speculation that she found frankly unbearable.

Ahead of her, down the hill, a thread of smoke was rising from a clump of trees. Houses, she thought with a quick thump of the heart. People. And among them would be Gethyn. So far she had refused to contemplate what she would say to him when they were actually face to face. The situation was a potential minefield, and she would have to rely on her instincts to guide her, although they had not proved to be very reliable in the past.

She drove slowly, telling herself it was because the road sloped steeply with sharp bends, refusing to acknowledge the emotional reluctance that kept her foot on the brake. But it was not such a terrifying prospect that faced her after all as she turned into the narrow village street. A handful of slate-roofed cottages facing each other. A post office, combined with general store. A petrol filling station and an inn. No estranged husband stood forbiddingly in the middle of the highway ordering her away. In spite of herself, her lips twisted wryly at the prospect. And the only dragon was a painted one—black with a fiery red eye—on the inn sign.

Davina drove carefully down the street. Some of the cottages had names, others numbers, but not one of them was called Plas Gwyn. And they didn't seem right either, with their lace-curtained windows and neatly kept front gardens bright with summer flowers. What part had Gethyn with all this quiet domesticity?

She licked her dry lips. Her obvious course was to enquire at the post office, but it seemed to be closed for lunch. That left the inn, which was a much more inviting proposition. She had been driving for a long time with no refreshment except a cup of coffee purchased in Shrewsbury. And a board outside the inn had mentioned bar snacks. There was a tiny gravelled car park at the side, and she drove in there. She leaned round to the back seat to recover her handbag, and took a deep steadying breath as she got out of the car. She pushed open the front door and found herself in a small lobby, with dark wooden doors opening on each side of her. On the right she could hear the soft drift of voices, predominantly male, with an occasional burst of laughter, and guessed this was the public bar. She opened the left-hand door and found herself in a small room, comfortably furnished with oak tables and high-backed settles. An old-fashioned wood fire had been laid in the grate but not lit. An elderly-looking golden labrador had been lying on the rug in front of the hearth, and as Davina came slowly into the room he got up ponderously and ambled across to put a damp but welcoming nose into her hand. Then he put his head back and gave a deep-throated bark.

'Quiet, you old fool,' a woman's voice called from the regions behind the bar. 'What's the matter with you?'

The curtain that hid the doorway through to the other bar was pushed aside and she came in, small and dark with glasses pushed up on her forehead. She put her hand to her mouth in mock dismay when she caught sight of Davina.

'There now,' she said. 'Me calling him names, and he was only trying to tell me you were here. What can I get you?'

'I'd like a lager.' Davina hoisted herself gracefully on to one of the tall padded stools along the bar counter and returned the woman's smile. 'And a sandwich, if that's possible.'

'More than possible,' the woman said briskly. 'There's ham, cheese or turkey. Or I've a menu somewhere ...' She began to fill a glass with lager, peering round for the menu card as she did so.

'Turkey would be fine,' Davina assured her.

'Come far, have you?' The woman set the glass down on a mat and pushed it towards Davina. Her twinkling eyes frankly assessed the classic lines of the cool shirtwaister dress, and the cost of the gold chain Davina wore round her throat.

'Quite a way,' Davina agreed noncommittally. The lager was ice-cold, frosting the outside of the glass, and she sipped it gratefully.

'It's chilly in here.' The landlady hunched her shoulders in a slight shiver. 'Shall I put a match to the old fire for you?'

'Oh, no, please.' Davina put out a detaining hand. 'It's a gorgeous day. Perhaps I could take a chair outside.'

'No need for that. There's a patch of grass at the back and a few tables. You can sit and look at the river and I'll bring your sandwiches out to you.'

'Do you get many tourists?' Davina asked, gathering up her handbag and preparing to follow.

'Oh yes. Surprising it is. Families, mostly, which is why I have the tables outside—for the children, see. Funny old licensing laws we have. And there'll be more visitors, I daresay, if the old mill up the valley gets working again as they reckon.'

'Mill?' Davina raised her brows questioningly.

The woman nodded vigorously. 'An old woollen mill. Very dilapidated, but they say it will work again. Fine thing, too, for Moel y Ddraig when it does. A bit of local industry to keep the youngsters from drifting away.'

She led the way along a narrow passage and flung open the door at the end.

'Through the yard, see, and round the corner,' she direc-ted. 'I'll bring your lunch in a minute.'

It was a wide lawn, sloping gently down towards the river at the bottom. Davina strolled down to the bank and stood on its edge, gazing down into the clear fast-flowing water. It was quite shallow at this point, but further out there were deeper pools and in one of these two small boys stood fishing happily. They gave Davina a friendly wave, and she waved back, suddenly enjoying the fresh sparkle of the water and the kiss of the sun on her face.

The sandwiches which arrived with amazing promptness were delicious—thick slices of turkey breast with a slight sprinkling of salt laid between chunks of undoubtedly home-made bread. The butter too had a taste which had nothing to do with supermarkets. Even the crusts were good. When she had finished, Davina sat back with a sigh of repletion. She smilingly refused an offer of apple pie and cream, but accepted a cup of coffee.

'You don't do bed and breakfast, I suppose?' She was only half-joking. It had occurred to her that she would need to stay overnight somewhere, and that the inn would make as good a base as any.

'I'm sorry, I don't.' The landlady set a cup of coffee down on the small iron table and added a bowl of brown sugar. 'But Mrs Parry might be able to help you, that is if she's not full up with her pony-trekkers. Are you going to be staying long?'

'I'm not sure.' Davina realised with irritation that she was being deliberately evasive. Yet what was the point? Sooner or later she would have to ask someone if they knew Gethyn, and this woman was friendly and approach-able. She hesitated. 'As a matter of fact, I'm here on busi-ness. I—I'm looking for someone—a Gethyn Lloyd. He's a writer.'

'Mr Lloyd—a writer? Well, there's a thing, now.' The

other woman sounded amazed. 'You won't have to look much further, though. He's up at Plas Gwyn. In fact, it belongs to him.'

'Yes, that's the place,' Davina said, relieved that her search was turning out to be relatively simple. 'Can you tell me where it is?'

'Why, of course I can. That's where I was going to send you for the bed and breakfast. It's Mr Lloyd's aunt, Mrs Parry, who does all that side of it, and young Rhiannon who takes out the riders.'

Davina smothered a gasp of disbelief. Gethyn might have his reasons for burying himself in the solitude of a remote valley, but she found it hard to take that one of them could involve the running of a pony-trekking centre. And she was frankly dismayed to learn that the only accommodation she could obtain locally seemed to be under his roof. That had not entered her plans at all. She had taken it for granted that any interview she might have with him could at least be conducted on some form of neutral territory.

It was on the tip of her tongue to ask the landlady if she could not make an exception and put her up for the night, but she stifled the impulse. Friendly she might be, but this was only a small place and gossip would be rife. Davina guessed her arrival and revelation about Gethyn's identity would be sufficient of a nine-day wonder without giving more grounds for speculation. And if she was only a business acquaintance as she had said, she had no real reason for rejecting Mrs Parry's accommodation. All she could do was hope that Plas Gwyn would be full of pony-trekkers and that there would be no room for her. If that was so, she would have to start for home again that evening and trust to luck that she could find somewhere to stay on the road. It did not give her a lot of time to see Gethyn and talk to him, and she drank the remains of her coffee with a sense of resolution. She had little time to waste. She paid her bill, and listened to the landlady's explicit directions on how to reach Plas Gwyn. She was thankful she had asked. Without them, she might have wandered round for hours, as it appeared the house itself lay at the end of an unmarked track which was unsuitable for cars. Pony-trekkers, she thought with a wry inward smile, must be an intrepid bunch!

She was so busy watching the road and looking out for the landmarks that would guide her that she quite forgot the implications of her visit. It was not until she climbed out of the car to open the big white gate which closed off the track that the old misgivings assailed her. She paused. It was still not too late to get in the car and drive away like the wind. Then with determination, she dragged the heavy gate into place behind the car and fastened it with the loop of wire provided for the purpose. She had the oddest feeling she had burnt her boats, as she set the car going again, bumping forward over the rapidly deteriorating track. She found the parking place the landlady had mentioned quite easily about half-way down. Three cars were drawn up there and a battered-looking Landrover. Davina parked her own vehicle and locked it after collecting her handbag and briefcase. Her suitcase she left where it was in the boot. Then she started to walk. The sandals she was wearing with their high wedged heels were not the most comfortable form of footwear for these conditions, she soon discovered. The track was deeply rutted and there were loose stones everywhere as an added pitfall.

Davina thought ruefully that she would be lucky to arrive at Plas Gwyn with her ankles intact, and was thankful she was not burdened with the additional hazard of her over-night case.

She rounded a corner and the house lay in front of her. It was a rambling two-storey building, half-timbered and obviously very old. Moss and lichen had gathered on the slate-covered roof, and the small square windows under the heavy eaves seemed to slant at crazy angles. It was very still, the only sign of life coming from the faint thread of smoke issuing from one of the chimneys. Davina walked forward uncertainly. There were two small lawns in front of the house, bordered by a low white fence. On one of them a cream-coloured nanny goat had been tethered and she looked up with bright, acquisitive eyes as Davina opened the squeaking gate and approached the front door.

The door stood slightly ajar and she pushed it open tentatively and went in. She found herself in a large square
hall. A wide staircase in dark polished wood curved away to
the upper storey on her right. The walls were panelled in
wood too, and there was a big stone fireplace, swept and
polished, its wide hearth filled not with logs but an attractive arrangement of dried grasses and leaves.

On the left a passage stretched away to the back of the
house, and around the hall were three doors, all tightly
closed. Davina looked around her a little helplessly. A big
oak table stood on the left-hand wall, holding a small brass
gong and what appeared to be a visitors' book. After a
moment's hesitation, she trod across to the table and
struck the gong lightly.

Almost before the echoes had died away, a voice behind
her said coolly, 'Yes, can I help you?'

Davina turned sharply, conscious of relief that it was at
least a female voice. The girl facing her was, she judged,
younger than herself, tall and slim with a cloud of dark
hair hanging on her shoulders. She wore a pair of riding
breeches, well-fitting but shabby, and a faded checked shirt.
Her glance, while not exactly hostile, did not reflect the
generally welcoming atmosphere of the house. It seemed to
assess Davina and then dismiss her.

'I'm looking for Mr Gethyn Lloyd,' said Davina.

'Oh?' The girl's brows rose interrogatively. 'And who is it
wants him?'

Davina hesitated. Her impulse was to tell this stranger to
mind her own business, but she controlled it. Judging by
what the woman at the inn had said this must be Rhiannon,
and Davina had no wish to start off on bad terms with a
member of the Plas Gwyn household. Things were going to
be difficult enough without that. She decided to play it
cool. After all, she had no means of knowing how much this
Rhiannon might know of Gethyn's private life or her own
brief part in it.

'My name is Greer,' she said quietly. 'Davina Greer.'

The girl took a step forward, and her eyes were blazing.

Davina felt herself recoil instinctively before this fierce dislike.

'Oh, is it?' she said with a kind of angry derision. 'Well,
you can just go back where you came from. You're not
wanted here.'

'Rhiannon!' The shocked protest came from the stairs.
Davina glanced up and saw they had been joined by an
older woman. It was impossible that she and the angry
Rhiannon could be other than mother and daughter. Mrs
Parry's dark hair might be silvering at the temples, and her
eyes full of anxiety instead of sparking with temper, but
their basic bone structure was practically identical.

She came down the stairs, casting her daughter a look of
dismay. 'I'm so sorry,' she turned apologetically to Davina.
'It's quite true we are full at the moment, but that's no
reason for my daughter's discourtesy.'

Rhiannon moved impatiently. 'You don't understand,
Mam. She hasn't come to stay. She's come to see Gethyn.
She's his wife.'

The last staccato sentence died away into an awkward
silence. Eventually Mrs Parry said nervously, 'Oh dear—I
wonder what . . . I suppose I'd better introduce myself. I'm
Gethyn's Aunt Beth—his father's sister.'

It seemed ludicrous under the circumstances to express
any kind of pleasure at the meeting, so Davina contented
herself with shaking hands in silence.

'I'm sorry if my arrival has upset anyone,' she said at
last. 'But I am here on business.' She indicated her briefcase, leaning against one leg of the table.

Mrs Parry eyed it almost distractedly. 'Yes, of course,
only . . . It's so difficult, you see.'

'Mrs Parry,' Davina tried to sound reassuring, 'I haven't
come to stay. I work for my uncle at Hanson Greer and I
have some papers for Gethyn to look at. If I could just see
him for a few minutes . . .'

'Well, you can't, then,' Rhiannon broke in rudely. 'Because he's not here and he won't be back until tomorrow
or the next day. So you may as well take yourself off.'

'Rhiannon!' It was her mother's turn to sound really

angry now. 'If you can't be civil, you'd better go to your room. I'll deal with this.'

Rhiannon's lip curled. 'Please yourself. If you want me, I'll be in the stables.' With a last inimical glance at Davina she walked out of the front door and disappeared.

Mrs Parry became galvanised into activity. 'Won't you come in, Miss—er—oh!' She broke off in confusion. 'I don't even know what to call you.' She threw open one of the doors on the left revealing a large sitting room furnished with comfortable sofas and deep armchairs covered in faded chintz. 'Do sit down. I'll go and make some tea.'

Davina halted her. 'Please—not for me. Was Rhiannon right? Is Gethyn not here?'

His aunt looked troubled. 'Well, no—not at the moment he isn't. He'll be back, of course, but it's difficult to say when. He comes and goes as he pleases, you see.'

'He hasn't changed,' Davina said quietly. She made herself smile briefly. 'Well, that makes things—rather awkward. I had rather counted on seeing him. My uncle will be very disappointed.'

Mrs Parry appeared to think quickly and make up her mind. 'Well, if you'd like to stay and wait until he returns, you'd be very welcome.'

Davina hesitated. It was obviously the most sensible course to pursue under the circumstances, yet she felt uncertain. For one thing she was putting Gethyn's aunt in a difficult position, and for another she would have to cope with Rhiannon's open hostility. Gethyn, it seemed, had not been reticent about the past with his young cousin.

'I don't know,' she said eventually. 'It's very kind of you, but I thought you said there was no room.'

'Oh, but you're family.' Mrs Parry gave a quick, rather shy smile. 'That makes all the difference. We can find a corner for you.'

Davina bit her lip. To describe her as family under the circumstances was pitching it a bit high, but Mrs Parry clearly meant well and it would be churlish to reject the relationship or the hospitality, so she merely thanked her quietly.

The room she was shown to was quite a large one at the back of the house, overlooking a small orchard with a glimpse of the river in the distance, and beyond that the steep outline of the mountain. It contained a wide brass bedstead covered in a Welsh tapestry counterpane, and matching curtains hung at the windows. There was a tall dressing chest in one corner topped by a mirror on a swivel, and a matching mahogany wardrobe on the other side of the room. There was a small table under the window and an elderly easy chair close beside it. The floorboards and furniture gleamed with polish and a faint fragrance of lavender hung in the room.

'It's delightful,' Davina said after the first appreciative glance around.'

'It's a lovely old house,' Mrs Parry agreed. She walked to the window and pulled back the curtain. 'Nice view, too. It's clear today, so you can actually see the Dragon.'

'What did you say?' Davina stared at her.

Mrs Parry smiled. 'Moel y Ddraig—that's what it means. The bare hilltop of the dragon, and there he is, the old thing.' She pointed upwards and Davina, intrigued, came to her side.

It was quite true. The enormous crag which jutted out above the house could, with very little imagination, have been a petrified dragon. It was all there—the great thrusting head with its menacing horns, and the long clawed foot raised threateningly just beneath it. And if you half-closed your eyes, the great shadowy bulk of the hill seemed to become huge spreading wings . . .

Davina wrenched herself back to reality with a jerk. She smiled. 'I hope he's a friendly dragon, otherwise he'd be rather too close for comfort!'

Mrs Parry's eyes twinkled suddenly. 'Well, he's never done me any harm. Now I am going to make some tea.' She paused. 'Would you like to have yours up here, perhaps?'

Davina guessed that Rhiannon would probably be coming in to have tea and that this was a tactful intimation of the fact, and she agreed. The prospect of seeing Gethyn again had made her more keyed up than she had realised, and now she felt almost weak from anti-climax. She needed to relax and unwind for a while, and it would be far preferable to do so up here, out of Rhiannon's hostile sight.

Mrs Parry hesitated at the door. 'I'm sorry Rhiannon's behaving like this,' she said frankly. 'But she is very fond of Gethyn—always has been. But she'll come round, I daresay. Maybe this is the best thing that could have happened.' And on that, she vanished.

Davina sat down in the easy chair and looked out on to the apple trees, their leaves moving gently in the slight breeze. She still could hardly believe that she was actually at Plas Gwyn. She leaned her head back on the cushions and closed her eyes, absorbing the sounds and silences of her new surroundings. She could hear the distant sound of the river, and superimposed upon it, closer at hand, the bleating of sheep and the sharp bark of a dog. Somewhere a horse whinnied with a restless stamp of hooves, and below her she could hear the homely clatter of cups and the rising whistle of a kettle.

Presently, when she had had her tea, she would walk up to the car and fetch her case. It contained her night things and a change of underwear, but little more, and she wondered rather restlessly what she would do if Gethyn's absence was a prolonged one. She sighed. That he would be away from home when she arrived was the last thing she had bargained for. It was almost as if he had guessed her intention and timed his absence accordingly, but that was nonsense, of course. He could have had no idea she was on her way.

The bedroom door banged open and Rhiannon made her appearance, carrying, somewhat surprisingly, a tray of tea. Her eyes lowered sullenly, and her lips set, she marched across the room and deposited the tray on the table at Davina's elbow.

Davina decided to try another friendly overture. 'What a charming room this is,' she commented. 'I hope I'm not putting anyone out by being here.'

Rhiannon shrugged. 'Only Gethyn, and he's not here at the moment, it hardly matters, does it? Who knows? When he comes back, he may be putting *you* out.'

The bedroom door slammed on her departure and Davina sat bolt upright on her chair, her attention utterly arrested by what the other girl had said. Then she jumped to her feet and went over almost feverishly to the dressing chest, tugging open a drawer at random. Her worst fears were confirmed. A pile of shirts, neatly folded and unarguably masculine, was revealed. The contents of the other drawers only served to hammer the lesson home. This was Gethyn's room.

A bright spot of humiliated colour burned in her cheeks. What could Mrs Parry have been thinking of? She must know what the situation was between Gethyn and herself—might even be aware that a divorce was projected, so how could she have put her in this room?

Davina swallowed and closed the drawers, backing away from them. Then she caught at herself. She was being utterly ridiculous. She would have to spend one night in this room—two at the most depending on when Gethyn returned, and then she would be gone. It would probably be never necessary for him to know that she had slept in his room—in his bed. And she was being foolish to ascribe any ulterior motive to Mrs Parry. Gethyn's aunt had obviously been disconcerted by her arrival and had probably reacted without thinking. Besides, if there was no other room available, what choice did she have? It was either this, or some makeshift on a floor somewhere—possibly Rhiannon's room, and Davina shuddered at the prospect. She was being hysterical, she thought. She should be thankful for small mercies. At least she had a roof over her head for the night.

But she still walked over to the bed and pulled back the counterpane. She relaxed perceptibly. The bed linen was crisp and fresh, clearly newly-changed. She knew, with an odd twist at the pit of her stomach, that it would have disturbed her to have to sleep in the same sheets as Gethyn had used, and she told herself defensively this was because he was now a stranger to her.

But she knew, if she was honest, that that was not her real motive, and she turned away sharply, forcing herself to go back to the chair and sit down and pour herself a cup of tea. It wasn't her favourite drink, but she supposed wryly it might help to steady her jumping nerves.

Her pulses seemed to be behaving most oddly altogether, and she made herself sit quietly, trying to regain her control of herself. Anyone would think, she told herself, that the door was suddenly going to swing open and Gethyn was going to be standing there—as he had been that night more than two years before.

Davina put up her hands to her face as if she was trying to blot out the images that presented themselves relentlessly to her teeming mind. But it was no use. She was incapable of stemming the flood of memory that rushed to engulf her.

The bed in the honeymoon suite had been a very different affair—a wide, low divan with fluffy lace-trimmed pillows and a magnificent gold satin bedspread. She had sat at the dressing table in the white chiffon of her wedding nightgown, brushing her hair with long nervous strokes. She could see the bed behind her in the mirror, and she was assailed by a terrible feeling of inadequacy.

The dinner in the hotel restaurant had been a disaster. Gethyn had retired behind a mask of cool courtesy, and it was impossible for her to reach him, to try and explain the fears and apprehensions which were overwhelming her. In the end, resentment had begun to burn in her, and she had become equally silent. She shouldn't have to explain; he ought to know how she was feeling. But sympathy and understanding seemed to be the least of his emotions. When they left the restaurant, he told her abruptly he was going to the bar for a drink, and wished her goodnight.

She came up to the suite alone, and looked round her desolately. It was all such a farce. The flowers were already beginning to wilt in the central heating, and the champagne remained unopened. She found some magazines on a table and sitting down on one of the sofas began to leaf through them, but the words and pictures danced meaninglessly in front of her eyes, and at last she threw them down with an exclamation of disgust. She glanced at her watch and saw that Gethyn had been gone for over an hour. Her temper rose. Well, he would not come back and find her sitting here meekly waiting for him!

She banged into the bedroom and closed the door. If it had had a key or a bolt, she would have used them. She undressed and showered in the luxuriously appointed bathroom, then put on her nightgown and the negligée which matched it and went slowly back in the bedroom.

She was feeling totally unnerved by the apparent *volte-face* her emotions had suffered, and all because of a few bitter words from her mother. Was it—could it be because deep in her heart she knew those words were true and that she had married a stranger? She shivered and laid down her hairbrush. Was it better, as her mother had always claimed, for love to develop slowly from friendship and trust and respect over a long period, or could it burst on the senses in a few short weeks with all the violence of an electric storm? Did Gethyn love her? He had never said so —that was when she realised it for the first time. She knew he wanted her, and had hugged to herself her secret joy in her own sexual power over him. But love was a different matter and one she had tended to take for granted. He wanted her, therefore he loved her, and it had taken her all this time, to their wedding night in fact, to realise that the two things did not necessarily bear any relation. This was what frightened her—this lack of spoken commitment which should have come, she thought, much, much earlier than the brief vows they had repeated that day. Sheer physical desire alone was too transient a thing on which to build a relationship which had to last for life.

Her eyes filled with tears, and she looked in the mirror at the blurred image of a girl, her body barely veiled by the misting of chiffon, traditionally prepared for a night of passion, and terrified. She tried to recapture the memory of Gethyn's mouth on hers, to remember the swift, vibrant reponse he had been able to engender from the day they had met, but there was nothing but chill inside her.

And at that moment she heard the outer door of the suite slam. For a second she sat tensely, her slim body poised as if for flight, only there was nowhere to fly to. But her door remained closed, and after a while she relaxed perceptibly. Gethyn, it seemed, had gone to the other room, as he had indicated before dinner.

She slipped out of her negligée and laid it across the dressing stool, then got into the big bed. She felt lost in the wide expanse of sweet-smelling linen, and she wished fretfully that she had some sleeping tablets so that she could blot out this whole disastrous night. Perhaps everything would seem different in the morning.

She reached for the button of the bedside lamp, but as she did so, a slight sound came to her ears, and she looked up to see the bedroom door opening. Gethyn sauntered into the room, and pushed the door shut behind him. His dark hair was damp and dishevelled from the shower, and he was wearing a towelling bathrobe, and Davina knew with a sudden tightening of her stomach muscles that he wore nothing else. He strolled across the room to the side of the bed where she was lying and stood looking down at her mockingly. When he spoke, she could smell the whisky on his breath.

'Good evening, lovely. And how are we enjoying our solitary honeymoon so far?'

She bent her head so that a swathe of dark auburn hair hung across her cheek like a curtain. 'Gethyn, please,' she said in a low voice. 'I—I'm very tired.'

'Tired, is it?' The note of exaggerated concern in his voice was almost more than she could bear. 'But I thought a headache was always the classic excuse—or does that come later in marriage? You'll have to instruct me—I'm new to these feminine foibles.'

She looked up at him in swift resentment. 'You mean I'm the first woman to refuse the great Gethyn Lloyd?' she could not resist the biting words.

'No, I don't,' he said softly. 'Because you haven't refused me yet, and you'd better not.'

A searing quiver of alarm ran along her senses, and this time she made no attempt to answer him.

His voice went on. 'For the past few weeks, you've been

promising me all the delights of Paradise. But at the same time it was made clear that you being an innocent virgin, and Mummy's daughter to boot, it would be at a price. Well, today I paid that price, and now you're going to keep your side of the bargain.'

'Gethyn—no!' She spoke then, her voice husky with suppressed tears. 'It—it wasn't like that, believe me.'

'Then what was it like?' he said gently. He took off the bathrobe and tossed it aside. 'You have a golden opportunity, lovely, to convince me, right now.'

She was cold and trembling as he took her in his arms. As his mouth sought hers, she turned her head away, and her body flinched as his hands began their long, slow exploration. After a time, he lifted himself on to one elbow and stared down at her averted face.

'Was it all an act, then?' he asked, his voice harsh. 'All that passion and promise? My God, you really had me fooled. Well, you're cast in a new and demanding role now, Davina, and I'm sorry if you don't know your lines.'

He took her with an insolent expertise, just short of brutality. When it was over, she lay very still, the first scalding tears squeezing from under her closed lids and trickling slowly down her face. She knew he had left the bed, and when eventually she opened her eyes, he was standing watching her, tying the belt of his bathrobe, his face sombre.

'Goodnight, Davina.' His voice was cool and cynical. 'Thank you for the loan of your body. If at any time in the future you're curious to know how it really should be between a man and a woman, you have only to let me know.'

'I hate you!' she whispered with passionate intensity. It might have been a trick of the lamplight, but she thought for a moment she saw him flinch. But when he spoke, the mockery was still in his voice.

'Do you, *cariad*? Then that makes two of us, because I also hate myself.'

He turned and left her.

She fell into a restless uneasy sleep just before dawn. When

she awoke, it was to the rattle of a breakfast trolley being
wheeled into the sitting room outside. She sat up, pushing
her hair back, and dragging the covers across her body as a
quiet knock fell on the bedroom door. But no one made any
attempt to enter, and after a moment or two she got out of
bed. Her discarded nightgown lay on the floor beside the
bed where Gethyn had tossed it and she kicked it out of
her way with loathing. She slipped a black silk kaftan
heavily embroidered with butterflies over her head, and
tugged a brush through the tangle of her hair. She looked
heavy-eyed, but no more so than other bride waking up
after her wedding night, she decided with a wry twist of
her lips.

For a moment she stood, nerving herself, then she opened
the door and marched out into the sitting room with a
defiant tilt to her chin. But the gesture was wasted, because the room was empty. And the breakfast in its silver
chafing dishes was quite clearly for one . . .

She poured herself a cup of coffee, glancing in bewilderment towards the closed door on the other side of the suite.
Presumably Gethyn was still asleep, in which case, who
had ordered this breakfast? Cooked food was beyond her,
but she took one of the warm rolls and spread it with
butter. When she had drunk her coffee, she got up restlessly
and wandered across to Gethyn's door. She stood for a
moment with her head bent listening for some sound of
movement, but there was none, and after a brief hesitation
she twisted the knob and pushed the door open. The room
beyond was also deserted, the sheets and blankets stripped
back, and the wardrobe door standing open, as if the
occupant had made a hurried departure.

Davina's hand stole to her mouth as the implications of
this burst over her. He had gone. But where? She had never
felt so humiliated. Even the degradation she had suffered
at his hands the night before seemed to pale into insignific-
ance beside this. She sank down on to the softness of the
carpet and stared almost unbelievingly about her. Nothing
could have underlined more bitterly the terms of their
relationship, she thought, swallowing. He had married her

for purely sensual reasons, and when she had proved a disappointment, he had decided to cut his losses.

Slow anger began to burn deep inside her. And what was she supposed to do? Go meekly back to her mother's house and admit that Vanessa Greer had been right, and that it had all been a terrible mistake? She would see him in hell first!

Within an hour she had bathed, dressed and packed and was in a taxi on the way to Gethyn's flat. It had already occurred to her that he might not be there, but the landlord lived on the premises and would have a pass-key.

But there was no need for this. As she approached the flat door, she could hear the sound of Gethyn's typewriter. She banged her case down and beat a tattoo on the door. After the briefest of pauses, the door opened, and Gethyn stood looking down on her. He did not offer any kind of greeting or explanation, but his brows lifted almost cynically at the sight of her.

'Come in,' he said at last. 'There's some coffee if you want some.'

Davina gasped as she dumped her case down on the sofa. 'Is that all you have to say?'

He shrugged, his thin dark face inscrutable. 'What do you expect me to say?' he countered.

She held on to her temper with difficulty. 'Well, some kind of apology might do to start with. Didn't it occur to you as you walked out this morning that I would be worried sick?'

'Frankly, no, it didn't. How very wifely of you,' he said smoothly, and she could have struck him. 'But it can't have been too traumatic for you as you knew exactly where to come to find me.'

'That's hardly the point.' Her voice rose almost to a shout. 'You walked out on me!'

'You didn't really expect me to hang around that gold-plated film set playing the doting groom to your adoring bride for the benefit of a pack of hotel staff—or did you?' He gave her a long hard look. 'I gave in to you yesterday only because it seemed to be what you wanted. Now I'm no longer sure what it is you do want. Except that it isn't me,' he added almost as a casual afterthought.

Their glances locked, but it was Davina who looked away first. She moistened her lips. 'So what happens next?' She tried to imitate his own casualness, but could not disguise completely the tremor in her voice.

He shrugged again. 'Life goes on.' He made a slight gesture towards the typewriter and the litter of paper that surrounded it. 'I've started work, so if you do decide to stick around, I'd appreciate it if you could keep quiet. We're low on food, so you could stock up on that if you felt like it.'

'You're incredible,' she said shakily. 'You don't really care, do you, whether I go or stay?'

'Oh, you'll stay,' he said. 'Until a more acceptable solution turns up. Where else can you go without making yourself a laughing stock? And it won't be for long, anyway. I leave for America in five weeks. I assume that you—won't be accompanying me after all.'

'You assume correctly,' she said between her teeth.

He nodded. 'Well, now that we've got that sorted out, make yourself at home. I'm sorry conditions are so cramped, although under ordinary circumstances that probably wouldn't have mattered too much. You can have the bedroom. I've cleared a space for your things.' He saw a flicker of uncertainty cross her face and his tone roughened. 'Oh, you don't have to worry. I meant what I said last night. Any future move will have to come from you.'

She picked her case up and walked through to the bedroom, slamming the door behind her with unnecessary force. There was a short silence, and then from the room behind her, she heard the sound of Gethyn's typewriter again, and she sank down on the edge of the bed and, burying her face in her hands, began to cry very quietly.

CHAPTER THREE

DAVINA put up her hands to her face and found that her cheeks were wet. 'Fool!' she castigated herself sharply, reaching for a handkerchief and scrubbing at her eyes.

It was madness, all this raking up of the past. What had happened between Gethyn and herself was past, done and quite irrevocable. She knew that. Why else was she here? By letting memory have its way with her, she was simply re-opening old wounds which she had wrongly presumed were healed. It was disquieting to discover how vulnerable she still was. The past two years of solitariness had simply spread a thin veneer of acceptance over raw and tangled emotions.

She got up restlessly and thrust open the window, staring up at the looming bulk of the mountain. Every scrap of reason she possessed was warning her to get away from this place—that now was not the time for her confrontation with Gethyn. She could leave the papers that Uncle Philip had sent and depart first thing in the morning, she told herself. She would abandon the idea of any kind of personal appeal to Gethyn, and leave all future negotiations in the hands of her solicitor. That was the most sensible course to follow and it always had been.

She went along to the chilly old-fashioned bathroom with its black and white checked lino and washed the signs of tension and distress from her face before venturing downstairs. There was an increasingly savoury smell coming from the back of the house, and she traced it down a flagged passage to a tall white door at the end. She tapped on the door rather hesitantly and peeped round it, to find that her instinct had been quite correct and that she was in the kitchen.

It was a large comfortable room, dominated by the big scrubbed wooden table in the centre, and the Aga range which filled an entire wall. Beyond the kitchen was a small scullery, and from this an open door led to the sunlit yard. As Davina looked around her, Mrs Parry came bustling in from the yard carrying a flat wicker basket of vegetables.

Her smile when she saw Davina was welcoming, but a little surprised too.

'So you're down. Supper won't be ready for an hour or so yet, I'm afraid.'

Davina shook her head. 'I wasn't looking for a meal,' she answered. She pointed to the basket of vegetables. 'Can I help with those?'

Mrs Parry looked doubtful. 'Well, it hardly seems right. Wouldn't you rather go in the sitting room? There's a wireless in there, and a few books, though we haven't a television. The reception isn't good enough and ...'

'Oh, please,' Davina broke in impulsively. 'You'll make me feel I'm being banished and'—she attempted a smile— 'you did say I was part of the family. Do let me help.'

'Well,' Mrs Parry capitulated, 'as long as you let me give you an apron to cover your dress. You could slice these beans for me. Rhiannon usually does them, but she's gone up to the farm to fetch me some eggs.'

'I see.' Davina was conscious of a feeling of relief as she sat down at the kitchen table and reached for the colander and the knife. She sniffed appreciatively. 'Something smells good.'

Mrs Parry smiled. 'Roast lamb,' she said. 'We don't go in for fancy dishes—just good plain food. That's what people want when they've been out in the air all day, and we've got quite a houseful at the moment.'

'Are they all trekking at the moment?' Davina asked, but her hostess shook her head.

'It's a rest day for the horses,' she explained. 'I think one family were going to Dolgellau for the day, and the others have gone up the mountain to the waterfall for a picnic. It's a good place in weather like this. There's a pool where you can bathe, and even a little beach. You'll have to ask Gethyn to take you there when he comes back.'

The knife slipped and Davina came perilously near to

adding a slice of her finger to the colander of beans. Now
was the time to tell Mrs Parry that she was not going to
wait for Gethyn's return after all. There was no need for
any detailed explanation, yet somehow she could not find
the words, and Mrs Parry was chatting cheerfully on about
local beauty spots, and the moment had gone. When the
beans were done, there was a mound of young carrots to
scrape and chop, and when these had been dealt with, she
relaxed at the table and watched Mrs Parry pipe whorls of
whipped cream around the edges of several enormous fruit
flans.

As she worked, Mrs Parry talked. Davina guessed after a
while that the soft flow of words had been prompted at the
start by a feeling of awkwardness in the presence of this
stranger niece by marriage, and that Mrs Parry was basic-
ally a shy woman, so she set herself to respond and draw
her out, and soon they were laughing and chatting together with the comfort of old acquaintances.

Davina also found she was learning a good deal of what
had happened over the past two years. Mrs Parry's late
husband had been a farmer until the economic difficulties
which had affected so many small farms had forced him to
sell up. A week after the sale he had collapsed with a heart
attack and died within a few hours. That, she discovered,
was when Gethyn had returned to Wales. In a matter of
weeks Plas Gwyn and the land that belonged to it had been
negotiated for and purchased and Mrs Parry and Rhiannon
were installed. Rhiannon had been an expert rider since
childhood, and the idea of capitalising on this expertise to
encourage tourists to Plas Gwyn had followed almost
inevitably.

Gethyn had returned to the States, but about a year
later he had turned up on the doorstep unannounced to take
his place as the master of the house and local landowner.

'I thought he'd soon get bored, after all that travelling
around,' Mrs Parry confided. 'But it seems not. And now
he's got the old mill to interest him. It was almost derelict,
but there was a lot of the original machinery still in it, and
he had experts down to advise him on what would be

needed to get it in working order again. He's done a lot of the actual work himself, helped by local labour.'

Davina's eyes were fixed on her wonderingly. 'He actually means the mill to produce cloth?'

'Oh, yes. It's been done before at other old mills. It won't be a large-scale thing, of course, but it's always an attraction for tourists and the looms can make rugs and tapestries for them to buy at the little shop they've built on the side. The old crafts are coming back into their own these days. Mrs Davies in the village had a handloom and she's going to give demonstrations on it when the mill is working again.'

'I see.' Davina was silent for a moment. She found the whole concept of Gethyn immersing himself in rural crafts a difficult one to grasp. He was a writer and had his own art to think about. Surely after the success he'd had, he couldn't have abandoned his writing career altogether, yet that was what seemed to have happened. In all Mrs Parry had said, writing had never been mentioned once, and Davina knew herself that people in the village seemed unaware that they had a celebrity in their midst.

This was not the Gethyn she remembered, she thought bewilderedly. He had had a ruthless streak of ambition which had caused him to pursue fame and money quite unequivocally. He enjoyed the status that being a bestselling author had brought him. So what was he doing here in this backwater involved in a venture which would probably end up making him a considerable loss?

She realised Mrs Parry was watching her curiously and flushed a little. She could well imagine the kind of speculation that must be passing through the older woman's mind. Apart from anything else, Mrs Parry must be wondering if her days as mistress of Plas Gwyn were numbered, now that Gethyn's wife had arrived unexpectedly on the scene. Davina would have liked to have given her some kind of reassurance, but it was impossible without discussing her real motive for coming to Wales, and that she felt she could not do.

So she changed the subject and began to ask about the

pony-trekking—the number of horses kept for the purpose, and the problems of organising such a venture.

She learned that not all the horses stabled at Plas Gwyn belonged to it, but were the property of the Morgan family who farmed nearby.

'Rhiannon had her own horses, of course, but they were sold when everything else was,' Mrs Parry said with a sigh. 'It was a great grief to her, and Gethyn knew that, so he went all over Wales tracing them after the sale and buying them back for her. They were all in the paddock at the back of the house waiting for her when she got here. I'll never forget her face and nor will Gethyn, I daresay. She always did think the world of him . . .' Mrs Parry broke off in sudden embarrassment as if aware that the tenor of her remarks was hardly likely to recommend them to Gethyn's wife. 'But they weren't enough, of course, for the pony-trekking, so Huw Morgan suggested he go in with her as a kind of sleeping partner. He and his sisters had always ridden, but when the girls married and moved away the horses were just there, eating their heads off.'

'It sounds an ideal arrangement.' Davina was not sure of her reaction to an implication that there might be a warmer than merely cousinly feeling between Gethyn and Rhiannon. She was a lovely creature with that wild, rather coltish beauty which, for Gethyn, would not be spoiled by hostility or resentment. She frowned to herself, realising now the probable reason for Rhiannon's overt dislike.

But it gave her also a glimmer of hope. If Gethyn was attracted to his young cousin—if he was already in love with her, then wouldn't he be more than ready to accede to the divorce? With a slight pang, she recalled the sensual pout of Rhiannon's lower lip and the fullness of her breasts under the faded shirt. Gethyn would be more fortunate with his second choice, she told herself. Rhiannon would not poison their wedding night with her qualms and doubts, but then she and Gethyn would not be strangers to each other. Perhaps they were even lovers already.

But a glance at Mrs Parry's serene expression and untroubled eyes told her that this could not be true. It was impossible that they could be carrying on such a relationship beneath this roof without her being aware of it, or even suspecting as much, and there was none of the guilt of hidden knowledge in her smile as she thanked Davina for helping her with the vegetables.

Davina guessed she wished to be alone to put the finishing touches to the meal and made a tactful withdrawal. Some of the guests staying at Plas Gwyn had returned while she was in the kitchen, and when she pushed open the sitting room door she seemed, disconcertingly, to be confronted by a sea of unfamiliar faces. But mutual introductions were soon completed and Davina found herself drawn into the general conversation. It was taken for granted that she was there on holiday like themselves and she was soon the recipient of a number of maps and guide books which, she was assured, would help her make the most of her time at Moel y Ddraig.

There were a number of games in a cupboard at the far end of the room, and before long she had succumbed to the lure of Snakes and Ladders with some of the younger members of the group.

'I saw a snake today,' said Timothy Fenton, a freckled eight-year-old, with a disarming air of earnestness as he slid his counter up the rungs of a ladder. 'I thought it was an adder, but Dad said it was only a grass snake.'

His tone made it clear that in the excitement stakes, grass snakes were virtual non-starters. Davina repressed a shudder.

'I'm not very keen on snakes,' she admitted, and Jenny, Tim's younger sister, sent her a grateful look. 'Are there many round here?'

'Millions,' said Tim cheerfully. 'But you're O.K. as long as you stick to the paths, or at least that's what Mr Lloyd said. He said snakes won't bother you as long as you don't disturb them by treading on them or anything.' Again the implication was clear that Mr Lloyd's words were law second only in importance to that of the Medes and Persians. 'We walked right up the stream to the waterfall. I wanted to go behind the waterfall to find the dragon's cave, but Jenny wouldn't. She spoils everything,' he added with brotherly candour, throwing a six.

Davina gave Jenny a sympathetic grin. 'Is there supposed to be a dragon behind the waterfall?' she enquired.

Tim nodded vigorously. 'When it's stormy, you can hear him roaring. Mr Lloyd said so, but Huw Morgan said it was just the wind blowing through a hole in the rock.' He groaned and rolled over on his stomach. 'Isn't it ever going to be dinner time? I'm starving!'

'Then starve quietly,' his mother put in sternly from her chair by the window. 'And you can't be that hungry. You ate twice as many sandwiches at lunch as anyone else.' She smiled at Davina. 'Don't let all this talk of snakes and dragons put you off walking up to the waterfall. It really is very lovely, and the pool below is marvellous for swimming.' She grimaced. 'I hope the cold water has done my bruises some good before we start trekking again tomorrow.'

The sitting room door opened and Rhiannon appeared. She had changed into a dress with a vivid print pattern and the dark unruly hair was tied back by a ribbon. She smiled round, managing at the same to ignore Davina.

'The meal's ready, if you'd like to go in.' She stood back, allowing the guests to precede her out of the room. Davina hung back too, wondering if she should follow. At last, Rhiannon looked at her. 'There's not a lot of room in the dining room, so Mam wants to know if you'd mind eating with us in the kitchen,' she said as if repeating lines she had unwillingly learned.

Davina smiled politely. 'Whatever's most convenient for your mother,' she replied quietly. She followed Rhiannon down the passage, and stood waiting while Mrs Parry bustled about with brimming soup bowls, looking hot and flushed from her exertions.

'Can't I help carry some of the things to the dining room?' she asked at last.

'No, thanks,' said Rhiannon, picking up a loaded tray and starting off with it. 'We can manage. We always have.'

Davina bit her lip at the snub which she supposed she had invited and kept out of the way until the main course had been served. The flans had been cut into generous wedges and pushed into the dining room on a trolley so that the guests could serve themselves when they were ready.

The food was as delicious as the smell had promised it would be, but Davina had little appetite for it. She was conscious all the time too of Rhiannon's resentful face just across the table, and that was not exactly conducive to the relaxed enjoyment of her meal.

The coffee stage had been reached, and the trays of cups and pots carried through to the dining room by Rhiannon, when the yard door opened and a young man walked in with a casualness which suggested he was sure of his welcome. He was tall with dark brown hair and laughing brown eyes. His skin was deeply tanned, and his teeth when he smiled were even and very white. He was smiling now as he looked at Davina.

'Hello.' His eyes assessed her quite frankly. 'Another visitor? When did you arrive?'

'Today, and she's not a visitor. She's Gethyn's wife from England.' Rhiannon had returned and slammed her empty tray down on the kitchen table with more force than necessary.

'Then hello again, Gethyn's wife from England.' His grin widened. 'No use waiting round for introductions, I see. I'm Huw Morgan.' He held out his hand.

Davina put hers into it. 'And I'm Davina Greer,' she said after the briefest hesitation.

'Professional name?' His eyebrows rose interrogatively. 'What are you—an actress? A model?'

She had to laugh, and shook her head. 'How flattering! But nothing so glamorous, I'm afraid. I'm in publishing. I work for my uncle.'

'Brains as well as beauty.' He sent a mocking glance towards Rhiannon. 'Gethyn seems to have all the luck.'

'Stop talking nonsense,' Rhiannon said shortly. 'Do you want a cup of coffee?'

'Of course I want some coffee, *bach*. You don't think I came here just to see you, do you?' His tone was openly teasing, but the black look did not lift from Rhiannon's face. She slammed round the kitchen, fetching a cup and saucer and filling it with coffee before dumping it unceremoniously in front of him.

'I don't think I'll come to this restaurant any more,' Huw Morgan called after her retreating figure as she went out to the scullery. 'The service isn't what it was.' He took an appreciative sip of coffee and smiled at Davina. 'Don't take any notice of her. Her bark's always worse than her bite, and something seems to have put her out today.'

'Yes,' Davina agreed drily. 'My arrival, apparently.'

Huw sent her a meditative glance. 'Well, that's only natural, see. Very attractive man, her cousin Gethyn. Bit of a Sir Galahad too—rescuing Rhiannon and her mother like that and buying back her horses. You couldn't really blame her if she took a bit of a tumble for him, now could you?'

Davina, taken aback by this plain speaking, glanced apprehensively towards the scullery door which stood ajar, but it was doubtful whether Huw's quiet words could have been heard by either Mrs Parry or Rhiannon above the clatter of the washing up.

She looked at him. 'You think that's all it is? A bit of a tumble?'

He set his cup down, his expression suddenly wry. 'I'm counting on it.' He gave her a considering look. 'Are you staying long?'

'No.' Davina shook her head emphatically. 'I'm leaving in the morning.'

'Without seeing Gethyn?'

'Yes.' She made herself smile. 'It's not essential that I see him. I only have some papers for him, and those I can easily leave.'

'Hm.' The considering look deepened. 'Must be very important papers if they brought you all this way from London with them. Wouldn't it have been easier just to post them?'

'I think that's my business,' she said tightly.

He grinned, unabashed. 'Of course it is, *bach*, but I have an—interest too, shall we say? And I'm sorry you're going for another reason. Good-looking women are scarce round this way and Rhiannon tends to have things too much her own way. A bit of competition would have been good for her.'

Davina held up her hands in mock horror. 'And they call this the simple life! I shall be glad to get back to sweet, uncomplicated London!'

They were still laughing when Rhiannon returned.

'What's so amusing?' she demanded ungraciously. 'Have you finished with those cups?'

'And the answers to those questions are "Never you mind" and "Yes",' Huw said pleasantly. 'I'm glad to see you're all dolled up, *bach*. I'll go and change and be back for you in three-quarters of an hour, right?'

'Why?' Rhiannon stared at him. She flushed slightly. 'I'm not wearing this dress for your benefit, Huw Morgan.'

'There's a pity.' But he did not sound too downhearted. 'I thought we had a date with a disco tonight.'

'Oh.' Rhiannon looked taken aback. 'I'd forgotten all about that, Huw. I'm sorry, but I don't feel like going anyway. I've got a bit of a headache.'

Huw shook his head. 'Sorry to hear that,' he said. 'I've been looking forward to it myself.' He looked at Davina. 'How about it, *bach*? Would you like to sample the local night life with me, seeing as I've been let down?'

'Huw!' Rhiannon looked scandalised. 'She wouldn't want to be bothered with all that old nonsense. Besides, you've only just met her.'

'Well, she's got a tongue in her head,' Huw said cheerfully. 'Besides, she's not going to have much of an evening otherwise if you're going to sit glaring at her all the time. She'd be much better off going out for a bit of a dance with me. It's all in the family anyway, in a manner of speaking.'

'She's not one of our family,' Rhiannon denied hotly, then turned away biting her lip.

Huw smiled across at Davina. 'Come on, girl, what do you say? If nothing else, it will give you something to laugh about when you get back to London—*My night with the*

Welsh peasants by Miss Davina Greer. You might be able to write a book instead of just publishing other people's.'

In spite of herself, Davina had to smile. 'I was really planning an early night,' she began. 'I've a long drive ahead of me tomorrow . . .'

'See?' Rhiannon cut in rudely. 'I told you she wouldn't want to know.'

Huw shrugged. 'Then I'll just have to go on my own.'

'No, wait.' Davina's voice halted him as he rose. She had no real wish to go the disco, although Huw seemed pleasant enough, but there was something in Rhiannon's attitude which stung, and she reacted impulsively to it. 'Three-quarters of an hour, you said? I'll be ready. I'm afraid I have nothing to change into, though.'

'You look fine as you are.' Huw's grin was both delighted and triumphant. He walked towards the back door, then turned. 'Sorry about your headache, Rhi. Hope it's better soon. See you presently, Davina.' And he was gone.

There was a short tense silence, then Rhiannon, her flush heightened and her eyes blazing ominously, flung herself into the scullery, banging the door behind her.

Davina was conscious of a feeling of compunction. It was wrong of her to become involved in whatever the situation was between Rhiannon and Huw, and the only excuse she could offer was that Rhiannon had asked for it. The fact that she was wearing an attractive dress indicated that she had had every intention of going out with Huw that evening. Davina could only surmise that her reluctance had been totally assumed in order to demonstrate to herself that Rhiannon had a power over men that she could exert when she wished, only it was a demonstration that had gone disastrously awry. Huw Morgan, she thought with a faint grin, was by no means a conventional young man, and if Rhiannon were seriously interested in him, she would have to change her tactics. All the same, she regretted her own involvement, and wished she had stuck to her guns and insisted on an early night. If she had had the wit to leave Huw and Rhiannon alone together, they would probably have resolved their differences quite amicably, she thought unhappily.

She hesitated for a moment, then got up and walked across to the scullery door. She could hear the clatter of pots and pans but no sound of voices. She knocked lightly and pushed the door open. Rhiannon was alone in the room at the sink, a tea-towel swathed round her waist. She looked round, pushing a strand of hair back from her face, and her expression became set and sullen when she saw Davina.

'I've got an idea,' Davina tried a tentative smile as she came into the room. 'I'll vanish up to my room out of the way, and when Huw comes back you can be waiting for him. You really want to go out tonight, don't you—and Huw only asked me for devilment, you know . . .'

'You don't have to tell me anything about Huw Morgan. I've known him longer than five minutes,' Rhiannon snapped. 'And you can stop playing the Lady Bountiful. I don't need the crumbs from your table. You go out with Huw tonight and welcome!' She grabbed at a piece of steel wool and attacked a pan with it almost savagely.

Davina lifted her shoulders in a brief, helpless shrug and turned away. She had attempted a friendly overture and it had failed.

After the warmth of the day, there was a satisfying coolness in the evening breeze from the mountain and Davina closed the window in her room before rummaging in her case for the black crocheted shawl she had brought with her as a wrap. She put it round her shoulders and went downstairs. There was a babble of voices and laughter from behind the closed sitting room door, and she sent a rather wistful glance in that direction as she walked towards the front door. As she reached it, Mrs Parry emerged from the dining room with a tray of glasses. She looked mildly surprised to see Davina obviously on her way out.

'Going for a walk?' she enquired. 'It's getting a bit chilly. Would you like to borrow a coat?'

'No, thanks.' Davina felt more uncomfortable than ever. 'As a matter of fact, I'm going to a disco—with Huw

Morgan. Rhiannon—didn't feel like going, so he asked me instead.'

'And you're going.' Mrs Parry's eyebrows rose on her forehead.

'Well—yes,' Davina said defensively. 'There's no harm in it. Huw seems a pleasant boy . . .'

'Boy, is it?' Mrs Parry gave a distinct sniff. 'And how old are you, I wonder. Twenty—twenty-one? Huw's older than you by at least two years. I'm surprised he should ask you —a stranger, and a married woman. I don't know what his Mam would say. And what will Gethyn think?'

'I thing you're making a mountain out of a molehill.' Davina lifted her chin a little. 'Huw isn't the slightest bit interested in me. He's only doing this to teach Rhiannon a lesson because she was playing him up.'

Mrs Parry shrugged. 'Then I'll say no more,' she said rather coldly. 'But I'm disappointed in you, Davina. This sort of behaviour may be all right in big cities, but it doesn't go down well in a place like this. Married women go out with their husbands here, or they stay at home.'

'I see.' Davina was stung to anger. 'Well, if I'd followed that rule for the past two years then I'd have been a recluse by now.'

'Well, the choice was yours,' Mrs Parry returned doggedly. 'It's a woman's place to follow her husband. Let him go off on his own and you're asking for trouble.'

'You're assuming I was even offered a choice. It's obviously never occurred to you that Gethyn might have wanted to be on his own,' Davina said recklessly.

'When he could have had a lovely thing like you beside him?' Mrs Parry said almost derisively. 'We've bred a lot of men in our family, but no monks. I don't know what went wrong between the pair of you, and I don't want to know, but I'll tell you this—going out with another man, even if it is platonic, isn't going to help. All it's likely to get you is a good hiding from Gethyn.'

She turned and walked to the kitchen. Davina opened the front door and walked out into the garden, glad of the breeze to cool her cheeks and her temper.

It was all very well for Gethyn's aunt to talk like that, she thought, seething. It was easy when you only saw everything in black and white, and it was only natural that she should take Gethyn's part. But then Mrs Parry had never woken up one morning to find herself alone with just three laconic words 'See you, Gethyn' scrawled on a piece of paper on the living room table. Nor had she lain in hospital, desolate and in pain after losing her baby, whispering over and over the name of a man who did not come and who did not even send her so much as a message or a kind word. But then what else could she expect? There had been few kind words between Gethyn and herself. Just a few fraught weeks together in the flat, sharing meals and avoiding each other's glances, building up to an almost unbearable tension as the days passed. She had been merely the housekeeper, she thought bitterly, except that no housekeeper ever went to the lengths she had gone to to avoid even the slightest physical contact between them. Gethyn had treated her with a kind of aloof civility, but there were times when she was only too aware of his brooding gaze following her as she moved around the flat—times when she knew with a kind of desperation that this inhuman situation could not go on for much longer.

And the really shaming thing was she was not at all sure what her reaction would be when the inevitable happened and Gethyn decided to reassert his rights as her husband. She had no doubt that he would do so eventually no matter what he might have said. For one thing, on a sheerly practical level, he could not be sleeping properly on that cramped sofa. She had considered on a number of occasions offering to exchange places with him, but she had kept silent, fearful of what such a conversation might lead to.

Because no matter how much she might insist to herself that their wedding night had been a degradation, that he had used her quite cynically for his own pleasure, all the time lurking at the back of her mind was the memory of what he had made her feel, however fleetingly. That was what she could not forgive, neither him nor herself. For a few brief moments, he had been the lover whose lightest touch could send the fires of rapture singing through her veins and she had been poised desperately on the edge of utter self-betrayal. She shivered when she remembered what it had cost her to lie unmoving and unmoved in his arms, unresponsive and rejecting until he had left her.

But then she had had fear and anger to bolster her up, to lend iron to her determination not to yield to him. Now, she knew that however bitterly she might regret her hasty marriage and its strange, hostile aftermath, she was no longer indifferent to Gethyn physically. It was humiliating to realise that a comparative stranger could have such an influence on her most intimate emotions, yet it was a fact that she faced each night as she lay alone in the darkness watching with heavily thudding heart the thin thread of light under the living room door that signalled that Gethyn was still wakeful.

What she would do when that door finally opened, she did not care to contemplate. There were times when she dreamed restlessly that time had rolled back a little and they were once more in the days before their marriage, when she had clung to him, breathless from his kisses, frankly expressing her longing by the sweet pressure of her body against his for the closest union of all. Then she would wake to find that her arms were empty, and there would be the feel of tears on her face.

With each day that passed, the trip to America grew closer. Gethyn said little about it, except to mention briefly the clothes he intended to take with him and brusquely request that she would have them ready for him. He was working very day, and she guessed it was another novel, although she did not dare ask. She had learned quickly that while she could tidy anything else in the flat, his work table was sacrosanct and must not be touched. So she washed and ironed and folded garments away in tissue in the big lightweight suitcases and tried not to think how strange it would be when she was quite alone in the flat, day and night. Whatever happened, she decided grimly, she would stick it out. She would not go slinking home to her mother

with her tail between her legs. She had paid a few visits to
the mews house since her wedding and Vanessa Greer's
glance had been searching.

Davina thought ruefully that Gethyn had accused her of
being an actress in their relationship. Well, where her
mother was concerned, she had put her acting ability to
good use. She was sure Mrs Greer had no conception that
her daughter's marriage was anything less than blissful,
and she forced herself to endure her increasingly acid remarks with smiling ease. But Davina was thankful that her
mother never suggested visiting them at the flat. Vanessa
Greer had an uncanny knack for detecting atmospheres
and diagnosing their cause. Coupled with that was her dislike for Gethyn which she had never troubled to dissemble.
Among their earliest encounters had been a dinner party
which Mrs Greer had arranged with the fixed intention,
Davina knew, of making Gethyn feel uncouth and out of
place. But she hadn't realised until the evening had already
begun just what her mother had in mind and when understanding dawned, she sat frozen with misery in her seat,
waiting for the inevitable explosion. But it had never come.
Gethyn had realised before she had that Mrs Greer's highly
polished dining table was a well-concealed chopping block
and had smilingly declined to lay his head on it. Instead he
had set out to charm her guests while leaving his hostess
in no doubt that her motives were fully understood. Mrs
Greer had concealed her chagrin well, but her feelings for
Gethyn had become even more implacably hostile. For
ever after she had referred to him to her friends in her
daughter's presence as 'the Dragon Man' or 'Davina's
Celtic barbarian', accompanying the hurtful phrases with a
little silvery laugh which should have robbed them of
offence but of course didn't . . .

If she as much as guessed at the real situation between
Davina and her husband, then the floodgates of all her
bitterness and resentment would be opened anew, and
Davina had felt wearily that she could not face that. After
all, it had been her mother's insinuations which had caused
all her doubts and uncertainties in the first place. All the

weeks before the wedding, she had turned them aside, armoured in her love for Gethyn, resolutely closing her ears to every barbed remark. But in the end, like water wearing away a stone, her mother's words had got to her, and just when she was at her most vulnerable.

Davina gave a shaky sigh as she walked slowly down the path to the garden gate and stood for a moment leaning on it. But would she have been so vulnerable if her feeling for Gethyn had not been based on a transient physical attraction? As it was, her mother had been right in one thing at least. She had known pitifully little of the demands he would make of her. She had been totally misled by the iron control of his wooing, had assumed he would be willing to impose the same sort of restraint on himself once she belonged to him. She could not have been more mistaken, she thought bitterly. Gethyn's treatment of her on their wedding night had revealed him as the barbarian her mother had always declared he was.

The sound of a vehicle making its way down the steep track towards the house roused her from her reverie and looking up, she saw a Landrover swing round the final bend with Huw grinning at her from the driving seat. He jumped down and walked across to her. He was wearing a light grey suit and his shirt and tie were immaculate, and Davina was conscious of a sudden misgiving. He looked older somehow and infinitely more sure of himself, and she hoped fervently that he wasn't labouring under any mistaken impressions where this evening was concerned. She had agreed to go with him, largely through a sense of mischief. The fact that he was an undeniably attractive young man had seemed unimportant at the time. Now she was not so sure. Then just as she was about to make some hurried excuse, the memory of the papers and magazines a friend of her mother's had sent from New York flashed back into her mind. Gethyn, sitting in a night club with a girl dressed solely in what appeared to be some gauze veiling with a sparse sprinkling of sequinned discs literally draped across him, and the insinuative paragraph that had accompanied it, and later the other pictures and stories about him and Lise

Adair, the star of his film. They had been 'constant companions' in the gossip column phrase, although Alec, his agent, had told her that it was all a publicity stunt. But then wouldn't he have been almost bound to say that?

'What's the matter, *bach*? You're looking a bit down.' Huw had reached her and was swinging the gate open. He jerked a thumb at the house. 'Been having a spot of bother?'

'You could say that.' She tried to smile. 'Shall we go?'

'Hang on a minute!' He put his hand on her arm. His eyes studied her. 'You look as if you've been having second thoughts. Would you rather give the disco a miss? We can just go for a drive and have a drink if you'd rather.'

'Oh, no,' she said hastily. 'The—the disco should be fun. I haven't been to such a thing for ages.'

And in many ways it was fun. It was a fund-raising event held in a village hall in a neighbouring hamlet, and there were young people there from all over the area. The music was loud and strident with an irresistible beat, and she danced with an energy she had not dreamed she possessed. Huw was not her only partner. After what Mrs Parry had said, Davina had felt slightly awkward as he introduced her to his friends, but apart from their evident surprise that Rhiannon was not with him, they accepted her unquestioningly. But there was a slightly different reaction from some of the older women at the back of the hall who were preparing and serving the refreshments. Davina supposed it was only natural that a strange face at what was a purely local gathering should cause comment, but she found their veiled scrutiny and the remarks in Welsh that she could not follow an embarrassment.

Although she could not deny that she had enjoyed herself and that the evening had helped put her personal problems which had threatened to become obsessive to the back of her mind for a while, at the same time it was quite a relief when it all came to an end and Huw was driving her home along the quiet dark roads. He negotiated the track down to Plas Gwyn with care and brought the Landrover to a halt at the front of the house which was all in darkness.

'I hope I haven't been locked out,' Davina murmured, staring up at the blank windows with faint apprehension.

'No chance of that,' Huw said briskly, as he helped her out. 'And if you were, I know where the spare key is kept. Don't worry so much.' He smiled at her. 'At least you don't look so much as if you were strung up on wires as you did when I came for you.'

'Was it that bad?' she asked lightly. The front door gave slightly under her hand and she gave a little sigh of relief. 'Well, thank you for a pleasant evening.' She held out her hand. Huw took it solemnly, but his eyes were dancing.

'I can take a hint,' he told her. 'But I don't need one. You belong to Gethyn, *bach*, and I belong to Rhiannon, even if it's a hard job convincing her sometimes. That's why I'm so glad you've come. She'll have to get some of her daft notions about Gethyn out of her head—and they are only daft notions. You don't have to worry.'

'No,' she said, 'I don't have to worry at all.'

'Right, then.' He leaned down and dropped a light kiss on her cheek. 'I'll tell you one thing—Gethyn's a lucky devil.' He gave her fingers a parting squeeze and walked back to the Landrover. Davina watched him climb in and start the engine and returned his brief wave as he drove away. Then she turned and went into the still house.

She stood in the hall for a moment, pressing her fingers against her temples. They were throbbing slightly—and no wonder, she thought wryly, after the strains and tensions of the day followed by the music and flashing lights of the disco. But she knew that unless she took prompt action, her head would soon be splitting. She felt in her handbag and extracted the tiny box of painkillers she kept there, then walked down the passage to the kitchen to get a glass of water.

She paused in the warm darkness, feeling on the wall for the light switch, but she couldn't find it, and after a moment she decided she could get her bearings well enough to find her way across the room to the scullery. She set off cautiously, stumbling slightly against one of the chairs which had been left out from the table. She was at the scullery door, her fingers already grasping the knob, when the room behind her was suddenly flooded with light. For a dazed moment, she thought that she had inadvertently pressed some delayed action time switch, and then she knew, as a cold fist turned in the pit of her stomach, that she was not alone. She turned slowly.

Gethyn was standing in the doorway, his hand still on the light switch.

'Good evening, *cariad*.' His tone made a mockery of the endearment. 'So we meet again.'

CHAPTER FOUR

For a long moment, Davina could not speak. The utter shock of seeing him when she had imagined that he was miles away was almost more than she could take. When at last she found her voice, her words were tense and stumbling.

'But I thought ... they said ... I mean, I wasn't expecting ...'

He lifted an eyebrow and his mouth curled sardonically. 'You weren't expecting to see me? Is that what you're trying to say? I can't imagine why not. I do live here, after all.'

She flushed vividly. 'Yes, of course,' she said almost inaudibly. 'I'm sorry—I've been a fool.'

His smile was humourless. 'What an admission—from a lady I remember as a paragon of chilly perfection—Mummy's little girl to her fingertips.' His eyes went over her. 'You've lost weight, Davina. It doesn't suit you.'

She made a weary little gesture. 'It's been two years. Probably we've both changed.'

He had, as she could see when she at last dared to take a good look at him. The harsh lines of his dark face seemed even more pronounced and there was a faint sprinkling of silver at his temples. But his attraction was undiminished, she realised with a startled pang. At once she was on her guard. So the confrontation she had feared had come to pass, and her second thoughts had come just twenty-four hours too late. But she had invited this by her foolhardy decision to come here, and now she had to face the consequences. Her head was aching now in real earnest, and she lifted her chin as she looked at him.

'I came to fetch a glass of water,' she said. 'May I get it before we talk?'

'Always assuming we have anything to talk about.' There was a note in his voice which made her flinch. She walked

into the scullery and turned on the cold tap, reaching for
a tumbler which stood in the drying rack. She filled the
glass, then opened the tiny gold pillbox and took her
tablets.

She had not heard him follow her and she cried out in
alarm as his hand came from behind and closed over hers
and the box it held.

'Tranquillisers or sleeping pills?' he asked grimly.

'Neither.' She tried to control her heavily thudding
heartbeats. 'Although I do have some sleeping pills—upstairs.'

Upstairs, she thought suddenly. My God, upstairs in his
room. He was standing so close behind her that she could
feel the actual warmth of his body. With a feeling of desperation, she hastily rinsed out the glass and turned away.
She wanted to get away into the kitchen where there was
more room—where she could put more space between
them. And heard, as if he guessed what was going through
her mind, his soft laugh, deep in his throat.

She walked round to the other side of the big table,
pulled out one of the chairs and subsided thankfully on to
it. Gethyn did not follow her example but propped himself
lazily in the scullery doorway.

'Well,' he said, 'start talking. It's been a long day, and I
wasn't expecting to have to drive back here tonight.' Her
startled eyes met his and he nodded sardonically. 'You're
quite right—a little bird did tip me off that you were here
and advised me to waste no time getting back.'

Davina dug her nails into the palms of her hands. She
knew who was responsible for that—and why. She wondered precisely what the message had been from Mrs Parry.
To hurry home because his estranged wife could be finding
herself a new boy-friend?

'It's not what you think,' she began hurriedly, 'Rhiannon
provoked me, I'm afraid, otherwise I would never have
accepted Huw's invitation.'

His green eyes widened, catlike. He lifted one shoulder in
an idle shrug. 'I wasn't aware I'd asked for an explanation.
You established a long time ago that you're your own—

mistress, and I don't imagine that chaste embrace I saw in the doorway just now will have changed the situation very radically.'

'Oh,' she said rather lamely, aware that her colour had deepened again. So he'd seen that, had he? she thought furiously. Wasn't it typical that he should be lurking in the shadows just at that moment? And she wished vindictively and paradoxically that she had responded to Huw's almost brotherly salute and given him something to spy on.

She deliberately choked back her resentment and tried for a businesslike tone. 'It must have come as a surprise to you to learn that I was here, but I do have a reason.'

'I don't doubt that. The only thing we might differ on is our versions of your reason. But go on, *cariad*, you have my undivided attention.'

'For once,' she muttered unwisely, and saw the green eyes flame suddenly, but his relaxed position leaning against the door jamb did not alter.

'Now you do surprise me,' he drawled. 'I had the strongest impression that my attentions to you were totally unwelcome.'

She stared down at the scrubbed table top, refusing to meet his gaze.

'I should be glad if we could remove this conversation from the personal level,' she said stiltedly. 'I don't see that any purpose will be served by harping back over old grievances.' That was true at least. All the memories she had evoked over the past few days had done was to revive an ache in her heart that she thought had been stilled for ever. 'And I'm here on business—strictly business.'

'Ah yes,' he said meditatively. 'These mythical papers from your uncle.'

'They're far from mythical!' She looked up indignantly. 'I can fetch them if you wish and then . . .'

'No, no.' Impatiently he waved her back into her seat. 'I'm not that interested. You can give me the gist of them, surely?'

It was an unpromising start, Davina thought ruefully. She said slowly, 'Well, apart from anything else, Uncle

Philip still has an option on your next book. The American market is clamouring for it, and he'd like to know when he can expect to see the manuscript.'

He said softly, 'Did he send you here to ask that? I would have thought an approach to my agent would have been more appropriate.'

Again she did not meet his eyes. 'Alec seemed to have no more idea of what you were doing than anyone else.'

He shrugged. 'Then that's obviously the answer. I'm not doing anything. Your uncle will just have to wave his option goodbye and tell the Americans there isn't going to be another book. Right?'

Davina got to her feet. 'It's far from right! You're a writer, Gethyn, and a good one. You can't just abandon a talent like that.'

'Watch me,' he said laconically.

'No!' She faced him her eyes blazing. 'You've created a public for yourself—a public that's waiting eagerly for more of your work. You can't just—betray them. It isn't ethical.'

'What an impassioned plea.' His voice was cold. 'Is your concern really with my readers or with Hanson Greer whose profits might show a decline without my continued services?'

'That's a foul thing to say,' she said jerkily. 'If that's what you believe, then break your contract. Offer your book somewhere else. Uncle Philip won't stop you.'

'I don't think he'd thank you for that suggestion. Philip Greer's a businessman, not a dewy-eyed philanthropist. Oh, don't get me wrong.' He lifted a silencing hand as she began an instinctive protest. 'I like your uncle. Of all the members of your family I've met, he's given me the least trouble,' he added cynically. 'But you'll never convince me he's going to quietly watch me change horses in midstream without lifting a finger to stop me. Anyway,' he gave a brief sigh, 'the question is purely academic. There is no book.'

She stared at him, her brows drawn together perplexedly. 'But there was,' she began. 'You were writing one in the flat—just before—you went to America.' She had been going to say 'just before you left me' and wondered uneasily if he was aware of her hasty substitution of words.

'What a memory,' he said admiringly. 'I'm afraid that particular piece of work died on me, and so did the spirit that moved it.'

She said haltingly, 'But perhaps if you looked at it again —it might have possibilities. That does work sometimes, you know—to give something a breathing space.'

'Is that a fact?' he mocked. 'Thus speaks the daughter of a publishing house. I always did wonder what you had in your veins instead of blood, Davina. It must have been printer's ink.'

The cruelty in his voice made her shrink inwardly. She forced herself to look at him, to lift her chin. She said deliberately, 'But what else did you expect, Gethyn? I did warn you that I was here on business.'

'Then I'm afraid your journey has been unnecessary,' he said, and his tone sounded bored. 'My writing career is over. I have other interests now.'

'So I've heard.' She dropped back wearily on to her chair. 'A woollen mill.'

'You sound disapproving. Yet the weaving of cloth is an older craft than the weaving of words, and probably far more respectable.' He came away from the doorway and walked across to the table, taking the chair opposite to her. 'Besides, locally, we need the industry, even on this small scale.'

'You said my uncle wasn't a philanthropist. It isn't exactly the role I'd envisaged for you either,' she said coolly, and he grinned.

'Philanthropy doesn't enter into it, girl. Other mills make a profit, so why shouldn't mine? They have a strong tourist appeal too.'

'And you really think you'll be satisfied with that?' she asked almost contemptuously. 'Selling tweed and tapestry to holidaymakers in this backwater?'

His brows rose. 'I'm sorry you have such a low opinion of it. I spent a holiday here myself once when I was a kid. Compared to the back-to-back houses and the slagheaps, it seemed like paradise on earth, and I knew then it was the environment I wanted for my own children.'

'Even with snakes on the mountainside,' she said with a wintry smile.

'Every paradise has its serpent. That's inevitable,' he said curtly.

Davina was silent. His casual reference to the possibility of children had discomfited her. It showed very clearly that he was looking ahead, beyond their broken marriage. She felt pain lash at her. How could he speak so casually when he knew that she had suffered all the heartbreak of an early miscarriage? That if things had been different and the baby had lived, it would have been walking by now—saying the first words which make those early years of the first-born so uniquely precious to its parents. She felt tears scalding behind her lids and dammed them back with a sheer effort of will. Gethyn might have been able to dismiss the conception and loss of their child from his mind, but she could not, and she swore to herself that she would never let him see the hurt he had dealt her.

She said tonelessly, 'I have something else to tell you. Apparently your last American tour was such an incredible success, they would like you to undertake another.'

For a moment he stared at her, then he began to laugh. '*Duw*, Davina. You never give up, do you? What are you going to tell me now—that I have a duty to the television networks and the luncheon clubs?'

She raised her eyebrows. 'You can't pretend you didn't enjoy the last one.' She hoped the bitterness underlying her words would escape him.

'Why should I pretend?' he shrugged. 'Being fêted and lionised on that scale is like balm to the spirit, and I was feeling pretty raw when I arrived in New York—for reasons I'm sure you'd rather we didn't go into.'

'In spite of that, it didn't take you long to find consolation,' she flashed, and wished passionately that the words were unsaid.

'Beware, Davina,' he said mockingly. 'A comment like that might make a more conceited man think you'd been jealous, and we both know that isn't true—don't we, lovely?' His voice had dropped almost to a whisper.

She moistened her lips desperately. 'You're being quite ridiculous. I—I think I'll go to bed now.' She pushed her chair back scraping it across the floor and stood up. 'I'll be leaving first thing in the morning.'

'Will you indeed?' He smiled faintly. 'Without even giving me time to consider your—interesting proposition? What would your uncle say?'

She paused, her attention arrested, in some bewilderment. 'Are you telling me that you—might be interested after all?'

'In the tour—yes.' He rocked back on his chair, his face enigmatic. 'The money would be useful for what I want to do here. Times are hard, you know. You could give me a couple of days to think it over, couldn't you? I'm sure your uncle would spare you for that.'

She bit her lip. In the circumstances, she knew Uncle Philip would encourage her to stay for as long as was necessary, and Gethyn knew it too. Besides, if she stayed, she might even be able to achieve her primary purpose for coming here and discuss the divorce with him.

'Or maybe you're not the businesswoman you think,' his taunting voice went on. 'I'm sure your uncle wouldn't run out on a deal simply because the going got rough.' His voice roughened. 'But that's always been your way, hasn't it, *cariad*? You lack staying power.'

'You say that—you dare to say that?' Her temper was rising recklessly. 'It was you that ran out on me, remember?'

'I've forgotten nothing.' He was on his feet too. 'It's all filed away—every look, every gesture, every movement.' His eyes went over her suddenly and she gasped. She might have been naked under his blazing glance. 'Every inch too.' He laughed savagely as he saw her face. 'Don't look so terrified, Davina. That's one thing two years of nothing but memories can do for you—it renders you immune. Now get along to bed—my bed—and sleep well. You can, for I won't be around to disturb your chaste slumbers.'

She stared at him, speechless with rage, her breasts ris-

ing and falling under the impetus of her emotions, then she
spun on her heel and almost ran to the door. She wrenched
at the handle, obsessed with the idea that in spite of what
he said, he was going to come after her—try to stop her,
but only his voice followed her.

'I advise you to stick around, Davina, in spite of everything. Who knows? You might get everything you came
here for. You're not the only one who wants to be free—
or did I forget to mention I'm planning to get married
again?'

For a moment she was motionless, rooted to the spot.
Then, forcing her suddenly nerveless limbs to action, she
very quietly opened the door and walked out into the
darkened hall. Moving like an automaton, she found her
way upstairs to the empty bedroom and went in.

There was a key in the lock, old and stiff, but her fingers
forced it to turn and when it was done, she leaned against
the panels of the door as if the effort had exhausted her,
closing her eyes wearily.

But this is what you wanted, a small insistent voice inside her reminded her. That is what you came all this way
to hear. He's going to let you have your divorce.

So there was no reason—none at all—why she should
suddenly feel so desolate.

The first thing she noticed when she awoke in the morning
was that everything looked grey. But as she lifted herself
up on her elbow, pushing her hair back from her face, she
realised that this was no reflection of her emotional state,
but simply that the weather had changed during the night
and it was raining. The second thing that occurred to her
was that someone was knocking with a certain amount of
impatience on her bedroom door and rattling the handle.

'Oh.' Davina threw back the covers and slid her feet to
the floor. 'Just a minute,' she called. 'I'm coming!'

She unlocked the door. Rhiannon was standing on the
threshold, holding a cup of tea. She looked furious.

'What kind of daft game d'you call that—locking your
door?' she demanded, thrusting the cup at Davina so that

some of the tea spilled into the saucer. 'Those ways may do in London, but we have no call to lock our doors round here. We aren't thieves.'

Davina met her angry look coolly. 'I never intended to suggest any such thing,' she said. 'Force of habit, I suppose.'

Before weariness had overcome her the previous night, she had lain awake for nearly an hour, Gethyn's parting words beating in her brain. She had been forced to the conclusion that in spite of what Huw Morgan might think, Rhiannon's feelings for Gethyn were not one-sided in the least. He had said he intended to marry again, and if there was another woman in his life besides his young cousin, surely local gossip would have picked up the fact by now. So all the indications were that he meant to marry Rhiannon, and it was essential that she conceal all traces of her confused and emotional state in Rhiannon's presence, and especially the motives that had driven her to lock her door the previous night.

For a long time she had listened for the sound of Gethyn coming up to bed, but she had heard nothing. Finally it occurred to her that she had no idea where Rhiannon's room was. If that was Gethyn's destination, and it was on the other side of the house, then it was no wonder she had not heard him, she thought. Certainly Rhiannon did not look as if she had slept very much—there were shadows under her eyes—but neither did she have the supposedly blissful look of a girl who had just spent a fulfilling night in her lover's arms. She looked totally out of sorts with the world as she flounced away, but Davina thought this was probably understandable. Her own sudden and inexplicable arrival must have jolted the apple cart to some extent. Perhaps Gethyn had had to spend some time reassuring Rhiannon that she had no need to be jealous—that he was in fact immune, as he had bluntly told her, Davina.

She sat down on the edge of the bed, shivering a little in her thin gingham nightgown, and sipped at the tea. It was comforting, in spite of the mess in the saucer. She glanced at her watch and saw to her surprise that it was after nine o'clock. She had slept for longer than she would have thought possible.

As she came downstairs, the pony-trekkers were just disappearing out of the front door, securely camouflaged in hard hats and voluminous mackintoshes, and they gave her a cheery wave as they trudged down the path into the mist and drizzle.

Davina went through to the kitchen. Mrs Parry and Rhiannon were both there, stowing quantities of packed lunches away in a pair of substantial saddlebags. Mrs Parry looked up as Davina entered and smiled rather nervously.

'Oh, there you are. I'll just finish this and then I'll make you some breakfast.'

'There's really no need. I only ever have fruit juice and toast in the morning and if you'll tell me where the things are, I can manage.' Davina kept her tone cool. She found it hard to forgive Gethyn's aunt for having summoned him home in such haste, and for such a reason. 'I'm sorry I'm late. I overslept.'

'Well, I would have called you, only Gethyn said to let you have your sleep, see?' Mrs Parry sounded flustered, as well she might, Davina thought grimly. It was a ticklish position to be in—with Gethyn's former wife on one side of her, and his future bride on the other. Mrs Parry gave her a sideways look. 'Did you enjoy yourself yesterday evening?'

Davina was tempted to reply, 'Fine—until I came back here.' But she confined herself to a noncommittal, 'Thank you—yes.'

Rhiannon fastened the buckle on the last bag with a vicious jerk. 'I'll be going now, Mam,' she threw over her shoulder as she made her way to the back door. Mrs Parry sighed faintly as it slammed behind her, but the smile she gave Davina was almost determinedly bright.

'It's been a busy week,' she said half-apologetically. 'But one family will be going home tomorrow, and I thought perhaps you might like to go out on one of the treks. There's some wonderful country hereabouts, and there's no better way of seeing it.'

Davina shook her head. 'I don't think so. I may well be going myself tomorrow, but even if I am still here, I haven't come equipped to go riding. And I'm not an expert rider by any means.'

'Oh, Rhiannon takes beginners too, and she'd loan you some trousers and boots, I'm sure.' Mrs Parry bustled about, cutting slices from a large loaf and putting them to toast, and pouring chilled grapefruit juice from a jug in the big fridge.

Davina could imagine nothing less appealing than borrowing clothes from Rhiannon, and decided that Mrs Parry was valiantly trying to convince herself that all was well, and that the undercurrents were all figments of her imagination. She contented herself with a brief smile and a rather sceptical lift of her brows.

Mrs Parry brought the toast to the table and began to ladle tea into a big brown pot.

'The best cup of the day, this,' she confided as she herself sat down. 'I like having the visitors—it makes the place lively, but it's nice just for a little while to have the house quiet again. What are you going to do with yourself today?' she added, putting a dish of home-made marmalade down in front of Davina.

Davina felt slightly taken aback. Mrs Parry seemed intent on treating her as if she was just another visitor to Plas Gwyn—a welcome guest to be cosseted and entertained. She was obviously determined to ignore the implications of Davina's presence.

During the long night, Davina had decided that she must talk to Gethyn again, and soon, however unpalatable the task might be. Hints and inferences were no good, she told herself. They had to sort out where they stood once and for all. In a way, things had already gone more smoothly than she had dared to hope. Perhaps today Gethyn too would be anxious to get their respective futures settled, without further recriminations on either side. Or was she asking for too much? she wondered wryly. She saw Mrs Parry watching her anxiously and gave a little start.

'Oh—today. I'm not sure.' She spread some marmalade

on her toast and bit into it with appreciation. 'The weather isn't really good enough for looking around the district, but I expect I'll just go for a drive.'

'If you're looking for the bright lights, Davina, you're going to be disappointed.'

She laid her piece of toast back on the plate, feeling her stomach contract painfully, as Gethyn sauntered into the room. He sent her a sardonic smile and reached for the teapot, filling a mug for himself.

'On the other hand,' he continued, 'I do have some unfinished business in Dolgellau. If you really want to play tourist for half a day, you could come with me.'

Davina hesitated. This was not at all what she had had in mind, but she knew it would be wisest not to allow that to weigh with her too heavily. Besides, perhaps Gethyn felt that they could talk more easily away from the house.

'Thank you,' she said composedly after a moment. 'I shall enjoy that.'

He lifted an eyebrow at her. 'Ever the optimist,' he drawled. 'Shall we say half an hour?'

It was not an encouraging beginning, but she nodded and gulped down the rest of her tea, almost choking in her anxiety to get out of the kitchen and away from him. This present confrontation was like a re-run of the previous night, and she knew she couldn't take it. On the other hand, what was she inviting by agreeing to spend probably the greater part of the day in his company? she wondered, as she gained her room. The face that looked back at her from the mirror looked pale and strained, and for a while she hesitated, her hand instinctively reaching for the blusher, but eventually she decided not to make any alterations to her appearance. She certainly had no wish for Gethyn to gain the mistaken impression that she was setting out to make herself attractive for him, she thought, and while she was about it, she scooped her dark auburn hair back from her face, and tied it at the nape of her neck with a wide black velvet ribbon.

When she descended the staircase, Gethyn was standing in the hall waiting for her. He had been smoking a cheroot rather impatiently, but as the stair creaked under her foot, he glanced up, his expression suddenly becoming remote and rather unapproachable. He was wearing a hip-length corded jacket over his faded jeans and cream roll-necked sweater, and the shock of his attraction lashed out at her again.

He looked her up and down. 'Haven't you anything more substantial than that to wear?'

She swallowed. 'Only the shawl I had on last night. I— I wasn't expecting to be here for longer than a day, and I didn't bring any extra clothes. And it was so warm yesterday . . .' her voice tailed away.

'Perhaps it was—yesterday,' he said grimly, and she did not deceive herself that he meant solely the weather. 'But any fool could see there was a change coming.'

He flung open a door built into the staircase revealing a crowded cupboard. After a moment's search, he produced a shabby parka and tossed it over to her.

'It isn't as elegant as your couture dress, but it will at least stop you being drenched,' he remarked expressionlessly.

Reluctantly Davina slid her arm into the garment. It was far too big for her and she guessed without being told that it belonged to him. The cloth still held the aroma of cheroots and the tang of some masculine cologne. The simple act of wearing it was almost like being in his arms, she found herself thinking, and the colour rose in her face. Fortunately his attention seemed to be fixed on the gloomy conditions outside and he failed to notice her momentary embarrassment.

He turned back abruptly. 'Ready?' He gave her sandals a derisory look. 'There's not much we can do about those, though I suppose the heels are high enough to lift you above any puddles.'

'I'll be all right,' she asserted, nettled at his tone.

'I'll take your word for it.' As she drew level with him at the front door, he reached out suddenly and drew the hood of the parka up around her head. His fingers brushed her face as he adjusted the hood and she pulled away as if she had been stung, biting her lip as she glimpsed the sudden savagery in his face at her gesture.

He thrust his hands into his pockets and strode out into the rain, his head slightly bent, and she followed, stumbling a little as the wet gravel shifted under her feet. In spite of the chill and the prevailing damp, the air was like wine and she gulped it in, glad of its cooling effect on her flushed face. What an idiot she had been to over-react like that! The last thing she wanted was to let Gethyn believe that she was still vulnerable where he was concerned. She had to admit that she had totally underestimated the effect on her that seeing him again would have. But she was here now and there could be no going back, so all she could do was carry out her self-appointed task grimly to the end.

Already his long stride was carrying him away from her up the track, and she had to almost run to keep up with him. She was breathless by the time they reached the parking place. Gethyn ignored the Landrover and unlocked the passenger door of a car standing nearby that had certainly not been there when she had arrived the night before. Davina thought ironically that she would have been bound to notice such an affluent-looking piece of machinery.

She lifted her eyebrows as she subsided into the cream leather seat, and he took his place beside her. 'Italian?'

He flicked the ignition. 'Yes—if it matters. You're surely not pretending that you're impressed?'

'It's not pretence,' she said frankly. 'But I didn't know you were particularly interested in cars.'

'I'm not,' he said briefly. 'It simply gets me from A to B a little faster, that's all. If you're a nervous passenger you'd better fasten your seat belt.'

She complied with the suggestion, giving him a slightly defiant look.

'It's nothing to do with nerves, merely common sense,' she said as the car made light of the track up to the road.

He gave her a derisive glance. 'So you're learning caution at last, are you? Well, I suppose better late than never. What a pity for both of us that the lesson didn't come a little earlier in life.'

'Before I came here, do you mean, or before I married you?'

He lifted an indifferent shoulder, as he turned the car economically out on to the quiet road. 'Interpret it whatever way you will,' he said coolly.

With a superhuman effort, she bit back the angry retort that was trembling on her lips and relapsed into silence. She had to admit that he was a superb driver. The travelling conditions were appalling, the rain and mist seeming to increase with every mile, and the road was narrow and winding, yet she found herself almost imperceptibly beginning to relax in her seat as if this was solely the pleasure trip it would appear on the surface.

'We're going by the shortest road through Llanmoel,' Gethyn remarked laconically at last. 'There is a scenic route over the mountains, but we'll save that for another day when the weather has improved.'

She stared at him. 'Precisely how long are you assuming I intend to stay?'

His mouth twisted in a faint smile. 'For as long as it takes,' he told her quietly. 'Wasn't that the arrangement we arrived at last night?'

'If so, I wasn't aware of it,' she said between her teeth. 'I was under the impression this was what this trip was all about—to get things settled once and for all.'

'Oh, did you?' His smile became satirical. 'Well, you can hardly blame me for your misconceptions, can you, *cariad*? But I'm not going to be rushed into any snap decisions, not even to oblige you. I don't consider I have any obligations where you're concerned anyway. I'll give your proposition due consideration—in my own time.'

Davina compressed her lips in ill-concealed irritation. 'Which proposition?' she challenged him. 'The American trip—or the other thing?'

'What a well-turned phrase to describe the demise of our relationship,' he said mockingly. 'Either, lovely, and I don't think it will do you any harm to be kept guessing as to which one it happens to be.'

'I have not come here in order to play childish games,'

she said tightly. 'Last night, you seemed to be in favour of the divorce—and you've had a chance to sleep on it. I don't see what . . .'

'The only thing I slept on last night was the sofa.' The green eyes were like ice as he shot a glance at her. 'It seemed just like old times—you in my bed, alone, and myself kept firmly at an uncomfortable distance.'

'Not always,' she said involuntarily, stung, and could have bitten her tongue out. She felt the mortified colour rise in her cheeks and gazed down at her clasped hands in her lap.

The silence seemed endless. Eventually he said very levelly, 'Very true. I was forgetting. It's good that I'm not a conceited man or I might fall into the trap of reading some significance into the fact that you remembered. So it really happened, did it, that night before I left for the States? I've often thought since that I dreamed it.'

'More like a nightmare,' she flashed, too shaken to consider her words.

Another silence. Then he said evenly, 'One more crack like that—just one, sweet wife, and I'll put you out of this car and let you walk—to the devil, if you want.' He paused, as if waiting for her to say something, and when she remained silent, he went on, 'You don't have to tell me that you hated yourself in the morning, Davina. That was one reason why I didn't wake you to say goodbye. I didn't want to take your recriminations on the plane with me—like so much excess baggage. Just for one night in your neat, tidy little life, you came down off your virginal pedestal and behaved like a real woman, and I knew you'd never forgive either of us for that. I hoped, of course. I even think I might have prayed at one point, but I knew all along how it would turn out.' He gave a sardonic laugh. 'I actually rang you from the airport before I left, but there was no answer. Where had you gone? Haring round to Mummy to show her the bruises?'

Her hands clenched together until she thought the knuckles would crack. 'Yes,' she said at last, 'I did—go round to my mother's house.'

To pack, she thought. To pack a lightweight suitcase with the sort of clothes that would see her through early fall in the States before she raced to the airport to seize the first cancellation, if not on his plane then on the one that followed it. Only when she had arrived at Creswell Mews, it was to find the doctor's car outside and the tearful housekeeper vainly trying to telephone her to tell her that her mother was asking for her. And all her lovely, shining plans had fallen in fragments about her feet because she knew that she had to stay, and as the days passed without a phone call or a letter from him, she began to tell herself that her mother's illness had been providential because it had stopped her sacrificing her pride for nothing. She had been trying to convince herself about this still when she had fallen downstairs. And after that she had needed convincing no longer.

The only way she could stop this tide of hurt and remembered pain was by anger. She clutched at it gratefully.

'What did you expect me to do?' she demanded. 'Sit alone like faithful Penelope until you deigned to return?'

'Hardly.' Gethyn pulled out to overtake a small truck, his lips tautly compressed. 'From what I remember, the faithful Penelope actually wanted her husband back.'

She began to tremble violently. 'Probably because she had something more than—brutality to look forward to.'

Gethyn gave a harsh laugh. 'Brutality? *Duw*, girl, you don't even know the meaning of the word! Just be thankful that I have an appointment in Dolgellau this morning or I might be tempted to stop this car and give you a practical demonstration of what it really means.'

She believed him. Her anger had lit the spark of his own and in this mood he would be capable of anything, she thought fearfully. And rejected with self-loathing the flicker of excitement that lurked there, suddenly, under the fear.

'I'm sorry,' she said in a subdued tone. 'I shouldn't have said what I did. It just proves that there's no point in trying to discuss things calmly. I—I was a fool to think there ever could be. I should have obeyed my own instincts and kept away.'

He shrugged, his face cynical. 'I didn't think you would have come of your own accord. Who persuaded you? Your uncle, or that smart solicitor you put on my track?'

'Oh.' She sent him a kindling look. 'So you did receive those letters?'

'Indeed I did. They went on the back of the fire,' he said coolly. 'His instinct seems to have been surer than yours, Davina. When I deal—if I deal, it won't be through a third party.'

Her heart gave a sudden painful thump. 'If?' she repeated bewilderedly. 'But last night you said you were planning to remarry.'

'So I am. But my—future wife is still rather young, so I'm not going to repeat past mistakes by rushing into marriage before she's ready,' he said dryly.

She would have liked to have raked her nails down that dark enigmatic face until she drew blood, but she controlled herself.

'Very wise, I'm sure,' she returned with deliberate insouciance. 'But are you sure she'll be willing to wait the further three years it will take for me to divorce you without your consent?'

He shrugged. 'That, *cariad*, is in the lap of the gods. It's a risk I'm prepared to take, so I advise you not to count any chickens for a while. As soon as I've reached a decision one way or the other, I promise you'll be the first to know. But for now, you'll just have to be patient—that is if you want the right answer.'

'Thank you,' she said between her teeth. 'Has it occurred to you that I might not have come equipped for a prolonged stay in this godforsaken place?'

His lip curled. 'You can hardly expect me in the circumstances to be acquainted with the intimate details of your wardrobe,' he drawled. 'However, it isn't an insurmountable problem. Godforsaken we may be, although I think our minister at Llanmoel would argue the point with you, but we haven't been totally deserted by retailers selling clothes. Naturally, they won't be the sort of thing you're used to, but none of your friends are likely to see you, and you can always send them to Oxfam before you go back to London.'

'Thank you again,' she said, quivering with temper. 'But I didn't come here expecting to have to go on a shopping spree either.'

He raised his eyebrows. 'Short of cash? That's no problem either. I'm far from penniless and I do still have the legal right to buy your clothes.'

'I'll see you in hell first!' she burst out passionately.

He smiled. 'Don't panic, Davina,' he advised with infuriating coolness. 'Just because I'm prepared to buy you a few clothes it doesn't necessarily mean that I intend to exercise any other rights—such as removing them at a later stage.' He pointed ahead down the road. 'We're nearly there, by the way. That great bank of cloud over there is Cader Idris. You can walk up there from the town, though I don't recommend it today.'

In a shaking voice she told him what he and the rest of the Welsh nation could do with Cader Idris. He tutted reprovingly.

'I hope you never use language like that in front of Mummy,' he observed. 'Shall I teach you to swear in Welsh while you're here?'

She didn't reply, but sat staring rigidly through the windscreen while he guided the car skilfully through the narrow, teeming streets. The traffic itself was heavy and there was the additional hazard of groups of people wandering along the pavements, stepping off into the road without looking when they found their way blocked. Gethyn seemed to accept the conditions without comment, so she guessed they must be typical.

He parked the car near to Eldon Square where the main shops were situated and gave her a sardonic look as he prepared to get out.

'I advise you to go to Griselda's for your clothes. She's an old friend, so you can quite safely tell her to send the bills to me. She can advise you where to go for shoes as well.'

'Thank you.' Davina gave a quick tight smile. 'Have you any other good advice for me before we part?'

'I have, but I doubt whether you'd take it,' he returned. He looked her over for a moment in unsmiling silence and then before she could move his hand had reached out and whipped away the ribbon that was confining her hair in one swift hard gesture.

'Oh—you——!' She put up a restraining hand as the wind took the hair which was now tumbling around her shoulders.

'That's more like it,' he said calmly. 'Or more like the picture of you that I used to carry in my mind—a long time ago. It's a crime to tie back hair like yours—like defacing some national treasure.'

'Very flattering,' she said curtly. 'But I don't propose to walk round looking a windblown mess merely to indulge one of your private fantasies. May I have my ribbon, please?'

'No,' he said pleasantly, 'you may not. And be thankful that I keep my fantasies private. The last time I saw your hair loose like that, it was lying across my pillow—and that was for real. So I should guard your tongue, *cariad*, or you might just provoke me to—realise my fantasies once again one night.'

He thrust the ribbon into his pocket, then turned on his heel and walked away, leaving her alone by the car with paling cheeks and parted lips as the full implication in his words came relentlessly home to her.

CHAPTER FIVE

DAVINA sat gazing at herself bleakly in the mirror. Now that it was too late, she fully realised the recklessness of the impulse which had prompted her action, but there could be no going back, she told herself ruefully, her glance going involuntarily to the floor beside her chair where the remains of her long hair was being swept up by a junior assistant.

But she could not complain that the new short style was unbecoming. The cutting had been skilful, and the feathery tendrils which had been coaxed across her forehead and cheeks seemed to accentuate the size of her eyes and the delicacy of her cheekbones. But there was no gainsaying that she suddenly looked younger, and that was something she had not intended, she thought unhappily. She had simply been determined to underline to Gethyn that any lingering proprietorial interest he might have in her personal appearance was totally misplaced. Now, it might seem just like a rather childish act of defiance, and, what was worse, she was already regretting the loss of her hair. She had acted on impulse, and the fact that the hairdresser could fit her in at once because of a cancellation had seemed at the time to confirm the rightness of her action. Now she wished she could have been given a breathing space to think again.

She paid her bill, tipped the assistant who had attended to her with a forced word of thanks and left the shop. She was glad to discover that the rain had almost stopped, although a light misty drizzle seemed still to hang in the air. She took a firmer grip of the parcels she carried and set out along the pavement.

She had found Griselda's without any difficulty, and had deliberately passed the shop by, although the cut and quality of the few items temptingly displayed in the window had almost drawn her back. Instead she had gone into one of the stores catering for the mountaineers and other adventure seekers who came to Dolgellau. By dint of using her credit cards, she had bought a couple of pairs of slim-fitting denim pants, some cheesecloth shirts and two warm sweaters, as well as a pair of tough canvas shoes. Later she had added a couple of the warm, hard-wearing fishermen's smocks on sale in the craft shops, and had supplemented her supply of lingerie.

She wandered along rather aimlessly, glancing in the craft shop windows with the rest of the tourists. It had not been until after Gethyn had disappeared that she had realised he had made no firm arrangements to meet her again. She supposed he assumed she would meekly return to the car when her shopping was completed to await his pleasure. Well, that would be the day!

Even the drizzle was vanishing now and in the sky a pale sun was struggling to make its presence felt. Davina discarded the parka with a feeling of relief that had nothing to do with the improvement in the weather. Perhaps a cup of coffee would cheer her up, she tried to rally herself, and help dispel this strange sinking feeling inside her when she allowed herself to consider what Gethyn's reaction might be to her rebellion over her hair. She compressed her lips. What could it matter what he said or thought about it? she told herself. It was no longer any of his business, and her action was merely a timely reminder of the fact that any relationship between them existed now only on paper.

She marched into a café and sat down at one of the tables with its gaily checked cloth, ordering coffee and a fruit scone home-baked and still warm from the oven. But delicious as it was, she might as well have been eating cardboard. Everything seemed to turn to ashes in her mouth. She had bought a guide-book to the area in a local newsagents and she began to turn over the pages, trying to concentrate on the information it contained, the history of the town little changed over the centuries, the fact that Owain Glyndwr had once held his parliament there in defiance of the English overlords.

She sighed and closed the guide-book, thrusting it into her bag. It was all very well for Glyndwr, she thought, her sense of humour unwillingly reasserting itself. He only had the English nation to contend with in his rebellion. Once, she remembered unwillingly, Gethyn had said that she could even make dragons eat out of her hand, but he had given no indication as to what would happen if she should be so foolish as to deliberately provoke one to anger, and in the dragon's own lair as well.

She finished her coffee, but no one seemed in a hurry to move her from the table, so she sat there quietly, her eyes fixed unseeingly on an oil-painting of the magnificent sweep of Cader Idris by a local artist which hung on the wall above her. There was a stark grandeur about Wales's high places, she thought to herself. Even in her brief sojourn, she could appreciate the overwhelming feeling of nostalgia for the mountains and valleys which afflicted expatriates. Perhaps Gethyn's return to the land of his fathers was more explicable than she had at first realised. If she was forced to stay for very long, she could see that she too might be caught in the spell of these wild and lonely hills, but even that might be safer than yielding to that frank bewitchment of the senses that Gethyn seemed to be able to kindle in her all over again. She gave a little shiver at the thought. It was all the doubts and fears that had taken possession of her on her wedding day and afterwards that she needed to remember. They were the reality. Not those few hours of crazy, soul-spinning delight that he had woven for her before he had walked out of her life without a backward glance.

Perhaps he had been realistic then, knowing in his heart that the sensual attraction which had brought them together was no lasting foundation on which to build a marriage. His second relationship would be based far more securely. Rhiannon he had presumably known since childhood, and there would be no unwelcome surprises in store for him after they were married. Davina supposed with a swift pang that they would continue to live at Plas Gwyn, and that their eventual family would be brought up there.

Pain struck at her anew as she realised Gethyn had never even asked about the loss of the child she had carried for him so briefly. It was all part of the same ruthless streak she had once found so attractive, she thought wearily. She had admired his single-mindedness, his ability to cut inessentials out of his life. But that was before she herself had discovered that she was one of those inessentials. And her inability to mother his child had only served to underline her uselessness in his eyes.

And as he had had no compunction in reminding her, she had not even got out of their marriage with her pride intact. In the end, his victory over her had been totally, shatteringly complete.

Her fingernail scored a crease deep into the tablecloth as unwilling remembrance of that night forced itself into her brain.

Gethyn's cases had been packed, and he was sorting through his papers, deciding what to put into his briefcase, when she returned to the flat from shopping. He had returned her greeting briefly without even glancing in her direction as she entered and she had walked into the kitchen, closing the door behind her with a slight slam. She dumped her loaded carriers on the table and regarded them sourly. So much for the impulse which had carried her into the food hall of a well-known department store! She had spent recklessly on food and wine, telling herself that she might as well splurge for one last time while she still had two of them to cook for. There was no fun and little point in making elaborate meals when one was eating alone. Or that was what she had told herself as she signed the cheque at the end. She had even bought a pair of miniature wooden candle-holders, and two long elegant red candles to put in them. Now she surveyed her purchases despondently and told herself she had been ridiculous, and also not quite honest. Why wouldn't she admit to herself that there was more to her motives than simply a future filled with solitary meals—that she intended to give Gethyn an evening meal to remember before he departed for the States the

next day? It would serve her right if she found he was due
to dine with Alec.

She unpacked slowly, putting the food away in the refrigerator. She wished she had simply bought something
unremarkable like chops. As it was, the meal she had
planned—a fillet of beef smothered in paté and cooked in
a pastry case—suddenly savoured too much of a celebra-
tion. That was undoubtedly how Gethyn would regard it
anyway, and she found herself wishing that they could part
without any of the barbed remarks and long electric
silences which had become a feature of their lives in recent
weeks.

Perhaps he would see it as a peace-offering, she thought,
trying to cheer herself up—a timid expression of the fact
that although their marriage had turned out to be a disaster,
she nevertheless wished him well—even wished that things
could have been different between them.

She stopped abruptly, her heart thumping suddenly. That
was something she had never admitted to herself before.
She had always explained this crushing feeling of regret
that had oppressed her lately by telling herself she was
mourning for the mess she had made of her life by her
reckless marriage. Now she knew that it was not as simple
as that.

Almost imperceptibly, she had begun to grieve over the
bleak facts of her relationship with Gethyn. During these
taut, uncomfortable weeks at the flat she had slowly begun
to recapture that overwhelming awareness of his maleness
which had been her downfall when they first met—had begun to listen with something approaching eagerness for the
sound of his key in the lock. It had occurred to her some
time before how quiet and deadly the place was going to
seem without the clatter of the typewriter in the living
room, a sound she had once dragged the bedclothes over
her head to escape. Now she knew how much she was going
to miss that particular piece of aggravation.

But at the same time, she was forced to admit that her
deepening regrets were far from being reciprocated by
Gethyn himself. His own attitude was coldly indifferent and

always had been. In fact, he seemed to go out of his way to avoid even the slightest physical contact with her, and oddly this was the most hurtful thing of all, though she had to admit that life in the small flat could have been well-nigh unbearable if he had behaved in any other way. Now, she found herself wondering what might have happened if Gethyn had once—just once—allowed that iron self-control he seemed able to assume at will to slip.

Her face flamed as the memory of their wedding night returned to torment her. It had been easy at the time to swear she would never forgive him for his treatment of her, but not so easy to maintain in the face of his own indifference. Whether she loved or hated, it seemed to mean the same to him. And as the hostile barrier she had tried to erect between them seemed to crumble, his own attitude remained unchanged. Her only crumb of comfort was the way he looked at her—sometimes.

She sighed, then caught at herself. If only she felt better in herself, she thought, then her prospects might not seem so bleak. As it was, the thought of having a meal to prepare was a nauseating one. For some weeks now she realised she had been suffering from a constant feeling of slight sickness, generally afflicting her at mealtimes. Obviously she had picked up some sort of lingering virus, she thought, resolutely ignoring the slight quiver of her stomach as she began to prepare the steak.

When she eventually went back into the living room to set the table, there was no one there, and she stood very still for a moment while disappointment lashed at her. Were all her painstaking preparations to go for nothing after all? she wondered despairingly as a mouthwatering aroma drifted after her from the kitchen. Then she saw the papers still scattered on his worktable and relaxed slightly, guessing that he had merely gone out to buy some cheroots.

She had laid the table and the candles were in place but not yet lit when she heard his step outside. She tensed involuntarily as the door opened. Gethyn walked in, then halted, his eyes sweeping the table and her own rather defensive stance beside it with frank irony.

'Expecting a guest?' He shrugged off his coat and dropped it on to the sofa. 'Shall I make myself scarce?'

She flushed and bit her lip. 'It was intended for you,' she said in a low voice. 'A farewell dinner. But it was obviously a bad idea, so let's just forget about it.'

She turned away towards the kitchen, anxious to hide the chagrin on her face, knowing too that her eyes had suddenly filled with tears.

'Wait.' He caught her arm, forcibly holding her back. 'I was just being bloody ungracious. I knew before I went out what you were up to, and it's far from being a bad idea.' He lifted a finger and flicked away the one tear which had escaped on to her cheek. 'So we'll call a truce in the cold war—just for tonight?'

The sudden gentleness in his voice was even more disturbing than his previous cold arrogance, and there was an answering shyness in the swift nod she gave him before she gently released herself and went back to the kitchen.

She was arranging the dishes of grapefruit and melon cocktail in the place settings when Gethyn emerged from the bedroom, stripped to the waist. He sent her a faint grin, pushing his hand across his chin.

'As you've been to all this trouble the least I can do is shave and put on a clean shirt in your honour,' he remarked as he disappeared into the bathroom. Her hands trembled slightly. Although they had been living here together, moments of such intimacy had been rare indeed, and a source of awkwardness when they had occurred. Now a sense of warm languor invaded her body at the sight of his bare skin and the memory of how it had felt against her own, and she gave a little gasp as the exact trend of her thoughts came home to her.

She was attending to the final dishing-up as Gethyn walked into the kitchen.

'Shall I open the wine?' He picked up the bottle and studied the label. 'Very impressive.'

'I hope you like it.' She thought miserably that the tremor in her voice must be as obvious to him as it was to her. 'I don't really know your tastes . . .' Her voice tailed

away as she realised that was not the most fortunate of
comments under the circumstances, but he did not seem
concerned, turning away to hunt in a drawer for the cork-
screw.

It was easier somehow when the meal was served and
they were sitting at the table facing each other. She found
he had switched off the pendant light and his desk lamp,
and that the room's only illumination was the flickering
candles. In a way she was glad of this, although it had not
been entirely what she intended. The moving shadows
afforded her a kind of privacy, concealing the unwonted
flush on her cheeks. Gethyn ate with appreciation, and she
was glad of it because her own plate remained relatively
untouched. She no longer felt sick—that, thankfully, had
passed, but the tension which had replaced it was in many
ways worse.

For dessert, she served cheese and a bowl of ripe plums
and grapes. The fruit was cool and refreshing for her dry
mouth, and she had begun to relax slightly as she got up to
make the coffee.

Gethyn's fingers fastened with unexpected firmness
around her wrist.

'Don't rush away,' he said lazily. She paused uncertainly.

'But the coffee . . .'

'Can wait. Why don't we finish this wine instead?' He
refilled her glass.

'Oh,' she said rather blankly. 'I didn't intend to have any
more. It goes to my head.'

He shrugged as he poured the remainder into his own
glass. 'Well, don't worry about it. If you pass out, I promise
not to tell anyone.'

Davina smiled weakly as she subsided into her chair. In
a way, she was glad she had the wine to blame for the sudden quiver in her legs and the strange lightheadedness
which was threatening to overwhelm her.

'I have to thank you, Davina,' he went on after a slight
pause. 'It was a—memorable meal.'

'Thanks.' She swallowed. 'I—I enjoyed cooking it.'

'It means I'll have at least one pleasant memory to take

away with me tomorrow.' His mouth twisted wryly. 'Generous of you—in the circumstances.'

She was silent, not knowing how to answer, reluctant to
look inside herself and acknowledge these strange new
emotions that seemed to be taking control of her. She tried
to tell herself that she had known the compulsion of these
desires and longings before—before she had married
Gethyn, and reminded herself of how ephemeral they had
been in the cold hard light of reality, when she had woken
from her romantic dream and faced the demands that he
had made of her. All the evidence suggested that a similar
disillusionment awaited her if she allowed her feelings full
rein once more.

She picked up her glass and swallowed some more wine.
Her throat felt dry and tight, and her voice sounded husky
in her own ears as she said, 'It's time I cleared away.'

'Leave it. I'll do it later.' His lips twisted at the surprised
glance she sent him. 'I am quite capable, you know. I did
look after myself here—not with the wholehearted ef-
ficiency you bring to the job, I admit, but then I never felt I
had to compensate for anything.'

'And you think that's what I'm doing.' Her voice shook
slightly.

'Well, isn't it?' he enquired ironically. 'Someone told me
once that the ideal wife should be a blend of a good housekeeper and a good mistress. Frankly, I'd assumed that your
efforts to outrival Mrs Beeton were motivated by a wish to
prove you could satisfy some of my requirements at least.'

'That's a foul thing to say,' she managed chokingly at
last.

'Is it?' He raised his eyebrows. 'I didn't intend it to be so.
I wasn't decrying your efforts. I'm very grateful to you.' He
gave a thin smile. 'I simply didn't expect that gratitude was
all there would be after a few short weeks of marriage.' He
pushed his chair back unhurriedly and stood up, looking
down at her flushed cheeks and shadowed eyes with something approaching compassion. 'I'm sorry, Davina. It's been
a delightful evening and now I've spoiled it for you. Get to
bed, and I'll deal with the debris in here.'

She muttered something incoherent and fled. For a long time she sat on the edge of her bed, her face buried in her hands, a prey to the conflict that raged within her. She might writhe with resentment at Gethyn's edged remarks, but at the same time she was forced to acknowledge that they contained a certain amount of justice. Her gesture in preparing the meal now seemed empty and shallow—a refusal to face the facts of their relationship. What had she expected him to think—to say? she asked herself miserably. Had she really expected to cloak the rift between them by showing that she could cook and knew about wines? They were the kind of superficial details that she knew would count for very little with Gethyn. In the weeks before their marriage, he had never even enquired if she could boil an egg, she recalled with a wry twist of her lips. Nor had she given much thought to the domestic side of their life together. It was all part of the same strange excitement that encompassed their entire relationship. It was the thought of living with him, of belonging to him, that obsessed her to the exclusion of everything else.

She gave a bitter sigh as she began to undress. What use was it remembering how it had been once? It was the present she had to concentrate on, and all its unassuaged bitterness. She slipped her nightgown over her head and walked across to the dressing chest to brush her hair, viewing herself with disfavour. Her cheekbones looked unwontedly prominent, and her eyes were as wide as a cat's. Her face seemed to be getting thinner in some odd way, even though she was acquiring extra weight she didn't want around her waist and hips. She bit her lip as she laid down her hairbrush. Didn't they say that putting on weight was the sign of a contented life? How wrong could anyone be? There was nothing even approaching contentment in her present existence, and when Gethyn left for the States tomorrow she would be totally desolate.

She lifted her hand to her mouth in a child's frightened gesture as she realised just what she was admitting, and all her incipient regrets returned in a flood to assail her. She could no longer banish the longing deep inside her to

know if there was anything left between Gethyn and herself.
She tried not to think about his overt avoidance of contact
with her, but fixed her thoughts instead of the times she
had glanced up and surprised him watching her. He had
always veiled his eyes the moment he sensed her awareness,
but even so ... The breath caught momentarily in her
throat and a long shiver went through her as she remembered what she had so briefly glimpsed in his regard.

She took a swift, impulsive step towards the door, then
made herself stop. It was very quiet in the living room.
The clatter of dishes and the movement of furniture had
stopped some time before. She had been waiting, she
realised, almost subconsciously for the sound of the typewriter to start again—her nightly lullaby, she thought half-
hysterically.

She stood motionless while her instincts fought a battle
with her reason. Once before she had allowed her uncertainties to acquire domination over her, and as a result
their entire relationship had been poisoned. Could she
allow the same thing to happen again? She pressed her
hand against her breast, trying to calm her hurried breathing.

Whatever else, she told herself, she owed it to them both
to try at least. Her legs were shaking so much she was
afraid they wouldn't carry her to the door.

Only the desk lamp illuminated the room beyond. For a
heart-stopping moment she thought he might have gone out
again, then she saw him. He wasn't asleep, as she had also
feared. He hadn't even begun to undress. He was simply
sitting on the edge of the sofa, his head bent. As the light
from the bedroom flooded into the room, his head came
round sharply and he looked at her, outlined in the doorway, his eyes narrowing in disbelief. There was a small
electric silence, then he said, his voice harsh and ragged,
'For God's sake, Davina, go and cover yourself.'

She took a quick, faltering step forward. 'Is—is that what
you want?'

'What I want doesn't enter into it.' He sounded unutterably weary. 'Let's just say I've learned to live with the

situation—up to now—but that doesn't mean I'm totally devoid of the normal human responses. Now, for God's sake go and leave me in peace before they get the better of me.'

Her hands shook slightly as she raised them to the nape of her neck, lifting the deep cloud of her hair slightly and allowing it to subside again on to her bare shoulders.

'That's what I'm counting on.' Her little laugh broke in the middle.

He was on his feet. Two quick strides brought him to her side, and the green eyes were blazing down into hers.

'You'd better mean that, Davina,' he warned huskily, then his mouth closed on hers with a devastating hunger. Just for a moment she was afraid again—afraid that she might not be able to satisfy the passion she had roused in him, then all thinking ceased and sensation took over.

Every inch of her body was awakening to vibrant, throbbing life under his seeking hands. When at last he lifted her and carried her to the bed, she was all eagerness, all desire. None of her wildest dreams had ever prepared her for a surrender so complete, or a pleasure so overwhelming. Just before she drowned in delight, she heard him groan something that might have been her name. Her own breathless moan of rapture was the only reply she could make.

Afterwards he lay for a long time without speaking, holding her closely against him, his face buried in the tangled mass of her hair. Eventually he roused himself, propping himself up on one elbow while he looked down into her face for an endless moment. Then he bent and kissed her eyelids very gently.

'Sleep now, *cariad*,' he whispered.

Submissively, she cradled her cheek against the warm sweat-dampened skin of his chest and closed her eyes. But sleep was not so easily summoned. The memory of the joy he had created for her filled her being, and she felt her throat constrict and two slow happy tears squeeze out from beneath her lids. She brushed them away with her fists like a child might do, refusing to let this delicious, languorous melancholy that was threatening to invade her take possession.

She let herself drift, savouring her contentment. And to-morrow, she thought drowsily, tomorrow she would open her eyes and Gethyn would be beside her, and they would talk it all out, and there would be no shadows between them again.

But when she eventually opened dazed eyes, it was late into the morning and the bed beside her was cold and empty. And the brief note propped against one of the new candlesticks on the dining table had been no consolation. None at all.

'Excuse me, but are you having lunch or is this table free?'

Davina came out of her reverie with a start and glanced up into the exasperated face of a woman standing beside her. Behind her, her husband and two small children waited patiently.

'I'm so sorry.' Blushing furiously, humiliatingly aware that there were tears in her eyes, Davina scooped together her various parcels and carriers and got to her feet. The café had begun to fill up without her noticing, and a small queue was forming.

'The idea!' she heard the woman mutter to her husband as she hurried to the door. 'No consideration, some people!'

When she gained the street outside, Davina paused for a moment, fighting for her self-control. Would she never learn? she lashed herself angrily. Was she some sort of masochist that she kept deliberately recalling this pain—this anguish? Surely she had suffered enough at the time. She didn't want to relive it all again. Nothing would change any of it, no matter how many times she beat herself with these memories.

She had to face the fact that however rapturous she had found that time in Gethyn's arms, for him it had been merely another sexual experience. She had known from the start that he was no novice where making love was con-cerned, and had suffered small agonies of jealousy before their marriage imagining him with other women.

Looking back, she could see that his masculine pride would have been affronted by her unexpected frigidity. Her aloofness and indifference to him would have been tantalising. But once she had yielded to him, she had become just another woman—and one that he had been forced to marry in order to win her. Now that he had won at last, what further allure did she have for him? She bit her lip savagely. Besides, her total inexperience had probably bored him. He was used to women who knew how to respond to a man, to arouse as well as be aroused. And in this, she had been signally lacking. Which accounted, she told herself painfully, for his cynical disappearance from her life just when, it transpired, she needed him most—not merely as a lover, though she was forced to acknowledge the multitude of nights when she had lain awake, aching for his caresses, but as someone to give her comfort and support during the ensuing loss of her child. Someone to alleviate the tragedy with his tenderness, to give her compassion as well as passion.

But in this, Gethyn too had been lacking. And this was why she had to make herself remember all the heaven and the hell she had known with him, to ensure that the incredible attraction he had always had for her did not seduce her into making a pitiful fool of herself for a second time.

It was all very well to tell herself bracingly that it could not happen, that she was free of him for ever. She had to admit that her awareness of him as a man was as potent as ever. Not even his callous treatment of her, and the fact that he had found another girl to share his future with him, could detract from it, and she was frightened.

With all her heart, she wished she had stayed in London and simply let the legal process run its course, no matter how long it took. Gethyn at a distance was easier to hate than Gethyn close at hand. Apart from anything else, he was the only lover who had ever possessed her, and that was, inevitably, a chain to bind her to him no matter how often she might tell herself that all fetters were broken.

Wasn't that why she had taken the drastic step of cutting off her beautiful hair—to prove to him that any physical claims he had on her were strictly in the past? She gave a slight shiver as she caught a glimpse of herself in a shop window. She looked like a stranger—and a nervous stranger at that. She couldn't escape the fact that Gethyn would be angry when he found out what she had done. And she couldn't forget the last time she had made him angry—on their wedding night, and the cool, utterly calculated revenge he had taken then.

She moistened her lips with a feeling of desperation. Well, the deed was done now, and she would simply have to face the consequences. She lifted her chin slightly, telling herself the worst he could do would be to deny her the divorce, and she doubted whether he would be prepared to take that step. After all, it was as important to him as it was to her.

Nevertheless, before she made her way back to where the car was parked, she went into a gift shop and hastily purchased a headscarf, which she tied over her shorn head. Her lips quirked slightly as she studied her reflection in the mirror provided by the assistant. As a cover-up, it was effective enough, but she couldn't hope to conceal what she had done under selected views of Welsh castles indefinitely. Sooner or later she would have to take the scarf off, but at least she had given herself a breathing space.

There was no sign of Gethyn when she found the car again, and she sighed in irritation. Then she noticed that a piece of paper had been tucked in under one of the windscreen wipers. For a moment she hoped vindictively it might be a parking ticket, but she knew there was little hope of that as the car was parked perfectly correctly, so she retrieved the paper and unfolded it. It was short and succinct. 'Meet me at twelve in the Black Swan. G.'

Davina almost ground her teeth as she crushed the paper in her hand. So that imperious summons was enough, was it, to ensure that she trailed meekly after him? She would see him in hell first! She took a firmer grip on her slipping parcels and stared around her. Common sense was telling her that it would be foolish to simply defy Gethyn for the sake of it and lunch elsewhere alone. She had to meet up with him sooner or later in order to get back to Plas Gwyn, and it might as well be sooner as later. She put up a hand

and gave a nervous twitch at her scarf. Or might it?

She turned and began to walk rather aimlessly back in the direction she had just come from. As she went, she began defiantly to justify herself in her own mind. After all, Gethyn couldn't be sure she had even received his beastly little note. It could have blown away, or been taken by someone else—or anything! And she had not the least idea where the Black Swan might be. She had seen various hotels on her wanderings, but she couldn't remember whether the Black Swan had been one of them.

She adjusted her parcels for the umpteenth time, cursing them silently under her breath. She had not bargained for having to wander the streets of Dolgellau laden like a pack mule when she had set out that morning. In fact, she wasn't at all sure just what she had bargained for. A chance to be alone with Gethyn, away from other eyes and ears in order to get their respective futures ironed out, she supposed. Well, in that case, the day had been a disaster. The businesslike talk she had envisaged had developed into something dangerously personal, and that must not be allowed to happen again. And really, there was very little to discuss. She would have to make it clear that she was not making any financial demands on him at all, and that all she sought was his consent.

She was so deep in thought that she almost screamed out loud when a hand descended bruisingly on her arm. She gave a violent start and her packages went cascading to the pavement. She looked up furiously into Gethyn's cool eyes.

'Look what you've made me do!'

He raised his eyebrows. 'I thought I was merely preventing you from getting lost. You're walking in the opposite direction from the Black Swan.' His voice was bland, but she was not deceived for a moment. He knew that she had not had the slightest intention of seeking him out. He had probably been standing somewhere watching her, and had seen her read his note and crumple it up.

She swallowed her rage, and allowed her gaze to become limpid. 'It's very muddling when you're in a strange town,' she acknowledged. 'And there are all these Welsh street names to cope with as well.'

'Poor Davina!' There was a marked satirical note now. 'And you with no tongue in your head to ask, of course. It was lucky I found you.'

'Yes, wasn't it?' she agreed radiantly, subduing an impulse to throw her remaining parcels at him.

He squatted down on the damp pavement, gathering up the articles she had dropped, his mouth twisting as the nature of her purchases became clear through the torn wrappings.

'Griselda mentioned that she hadn't seen you,' he commented as he stood up.

She bit her lip. 'I don't require a *couture* wardrobe,' she informed him stiffly. 'Just a few oddments to get me through the next day or two.'

He gave the assortment he had rescued a sardonic look. 'Oddments would seem to be the right word.' His glance went to the scarf she was wearing and he gave a perceptible wince. 'I see you've taken the role of tourist to heart. I had no idea you had such a devotion to castles. Remind me to take you to Caenarfon one day. It looks much better in stone, I promise you.'

'I doubt if I shall be here that long,' she said between her teeth.

'I'm sorry to hear that,' he said in a voice of total indifference. 'I hope you'll delay your departure for long enough to have lunch with me. I'm starving.'

He set off along the pavement with his long easy stride, leaving her to follow in his wake at an undignified trot. She was seething when she caught him up at the car.

'I think we'll dump these here,' he remarked, his tone suggesting he could suggest an even more appropriate repository. 'Unless you want to eat, swathed in denim and cheesecloth.' He unlocked the door and tossed the parcels on to the seat. Davina made no attempt to argue. She was glad to see the back of them.

A few tables had been set on the pavement outside the Black Swan, and these were already occupied by hardy souls, enjoying the pale sunlight. Gethyn swept her past them and into the hotel's main entrance. A glass door on the right admitted them to a small cocktail bar, and beyond Davina could see the restaurant.

He gave her an interrogative glance. 'Is it still Campari and soda?'

'Yes,' she said, and could not resist adding, 'You have a good memory for details.'

He gave her a thin smile. 'Not merely for details, Davina,' he told her before turning to the barman to give their order. There was a leather-bound menu lying on the bar and he handed it to her.

'I can recommend the steak and kidney pie,' he commented.

She ran an indifferent glance down the list of food. 'I'll have chicken salad.'

He tutted mockingly. 'You won't change those angles of yours back to curves on a salad diet, *cariad*.'

'Please don't call me that,' she said tautly. 'And I think my figure is my own concern.'

His smile widened. 'I doubt if anyone else would be much interested in it at the moment,' he said gently and unforgivably. Davina dug her nails into the palms of her hands, refusing to let herself rise to his baiting. After all, she reminded herself, the last thing she wanted was for him to become interested in her physical appearance.

She sipped at her drink, glancing around her. There were few other people in the bar apart from themselves, and she was far too aware of the tall man at her side to be able to take much interest in anyone else. With a pang, she remembered the game they had played in bars and hotels during their courtship, making absurd guesses about the identities and occupations of other guests, revelling in each other's laughter. Whereas now ... Her hand shook suddenly and she put her glass down hurriedly on the bar, aware that some of the dark pink liquid had splashed on to her dress.

'Oh, damn!' She scrubbed at the offending mark with her handkerchief.

Gethyn's hand closed over hers. 'Relax, Davina,' he advised softly. 'You're behaving as if you're strung up on wires. People are watching us.'

'I'm sorry.' She thrust the handkerchief back into her bag. 'But this is hardly a normal situation, is it? And I'm surprised you're so sensitive about being under public scrutiny. There was a time when you weren't so concerned with personal privacy.'

'Perhaps because I was too concerned with other things.' His tone was edged. 'But that no longer applies. If you want a scene, I'll oblige you. But not here. The owner happens to be a friend of mine.'

She sent him a glittering smile. 'You're very protective about your friends, Gethyn. Is this a new trait?'

'One of many.' His eyes were like chips of green ice. 'But I haven't changed in one thing, Davina. I still believe that a lot of women would be improved by a bloody good hiding, and you'd come top of the list.'

His voice was too quiet for anyone else to have overheard, she knew, but she could not prevent a wave of colour flooding her face. She was thankful to her heart to see the head waiter heading in their direction to take their order.

When he had gone, she said in a low voice, 'Gethyn, it's foolish to go on like this. Can't—can't we call a truce at least for the rest of the day?'

He sent her a derisive look. 'We could always try. But I advise you not to provoke me again, Davina.'

'No,' she said, unhappily aware of her shorn hair and resisting the impulse to make yet another nervous adjustment to her scarf. The last thing she wanted was to draw his attention again to her peculiar choice of headgear. She glanced round hastily. 'I—I wonder who all these people are. That group in the corner are climbers, of course, but that woman at the table against the wall looks rather strange. I wonder why she's wearing a cloak. Do you think she's an artist or just pretending . . .' Her halting words died away as her eyes met his blazing with anger.

His fingers closed round her wrist in an ungentle grip.

'What are you trying to do, Davina?' he demanded in an undertone. 'Pretend that the last two years have never happened? Well, I'll go along with you. Play your little games, if you must, but don't complain if you should find I've substituted my own rules.'

'I—I didn't mean it like that.' She lifted her shoulders unhappily. 'I was just—trying to make conversation, that's all.'

He gave a mirthless smile. 'If anyone had told me I'd ever hear you say that . . .' he said quietly.

'Please,' she said with difficulty. 'My wrist. You're hurting it.'

He released her almost contemptuously. 'Pity it wasn't your neck.' He swallowed the remains of his drink with one violent movement, and turned away. 'They're ready for us in the dining room.'

It was an uncomfortable meal. Davina barely touched the melon she had chosen as her first course, and picked at the delicious-looking salad when it arrived. It was little consolation to note that Gethyn seemed to have no better appetite himself, and she felt nothing but relief when, after she had declined a sweet and coffee, he sent for the bill.

When they were outside again, she touched his arm rather timidly. 'Are we going home now?'

He sent her a cool, unreadable glance. 'We're going to Plas Gwyn, certainly,' he replied, and she flushed at her slip of the tongue.

She kept silent as the car threaded its way through the busy streets. When they were clear of the town at last, she said, 'It was a mistake for me to come here, Gethyn. I'll pack up as soon as we get back. I'll go back to London and leave you in peace.' She stared down at her clasped hands. 'You can contact Uncle Phil with your decision about the trip—when it's convenient.'

She gave him a swift, sideways glance, but although his mouth tightened, he made no attempt to reply. She leaned back in her seat and closed her eyes. So that was that, she thought. She would leave tomorrow without having achieved any of the things she had come for. All she had

succeeded in was a further deterioration in the relationship
between Gethyn and herself. She stifled a sigh. It had been
madness, of course, to imagine she could arrive at an amicable solution to their problems with this—dark dragon of
a man. Gethyn was a law unto himself and always had been.

She kept her eyes determinedly closed. It was bad enough
having to sit beside him in the car, their sleeves practically
brushing, but at least she did not have to look at him, see
his lean brown fingers gripping the wheel and remember
the utter magic of their lingering, sensuous exploration of
her body.

When at last he spoke, his words seemed flung at her
like stones. 'You'll leave when I say you may and not before.
If you insist on going now, then I'll contest each and every
effort you make to divorce me for the rest of our lives.'

'But that's ridiculous,' she protested, her voice quivering. She sat bolt upright in the seat, her eyes fixed on him
appealingly. 'You want to be free as much as I do, and
besides—there's your bride-to-be. Aren't you going to
consider her?'

He gave a cynical shrug. 'I don't doubt I can—persuade
her to fall in with my wishes. Not all women are as insistent on the wedding ceremony as you were.'

She paused, her heart thudding painfully, then she said
in a low voice:

'You seem very sure of yourself.'

'Not of myself. Of her.'

'She has my sympathy,' Davina said with difficulty.

'She doesn't need it.' He slanted a look at her. 'I intend
to spend every moment that's left to me in making her
happy.'

A sudden searing vision of Rhiannon, her full mouth
parted in a triumphant smile, was imprinted on her inner
vision. She was horrified at the sudden, sick jealousy that
clawed at her throat.

But it made her reckless. 'Are you sure you know what
it takes to make a woman happy? You haven't been con-
spicuously successful so far.'

As soon as the words were uttered, she knew she had

gone too far. She blenched under the hard glitter of the look he turned on her, and an apprehensive shiver ran along her nerve endings as she realised he was bringing the car to a halt at the side of the road.

'Gethyn,' she protested, dry-mouthed, as he switched off the engine and turned to her. 'I'm sorry. I didn't mean it . . . I . . .'

Her words were crushed under the brutal pressure of his mouth. Her hands came up to thrust him away, and were trapped between their bodies as he pulled her against him so hard that the breath was jerked out of her. But she resisted him, mouth and teeth locked against his savage insistence, fighting the terrifying clamour of her senses, her body's instinctive welcome for him.

Just before her thoughts dissolved into chaos, she seemed to hear a voice inside her head screaming, 'No. No!' And as if he had heard the silent plea and knew that it was not a rejection of his kiss but only the desire to punish which had inspired it, his lips gentled suddenly, magically, and she was lost.

His mouth moved on hers, warmly and seductively, coaxing from her the response that force had denied him. His tongue flickered like fire over the curve of her parted lips before exploring the warmth and sweetness she had yielded to him. Her submission was total. She knew that, even as the sweet bright flame grew within her in answer to this remembered intimacy. Gethyn, after all, had taught her what a kiss should be.

When at last he raised his head, his breathing was hurried, his eyes as they held hers, oddly brilliant. Slowly, as if all the time in the world was at his disposal, oblivious of their surroundings, he pulled her down so that she was lying half across him, her head tilted back over his arm. His fingers brushed her lips in a featherlight caress, then began to stroke the smooth line of her throat. It was heaven, but it was not enough, and her body began to arch itself towards him of its own volition.

He gave a soft groan and his fingers slid compulsively under the neckline of her dress, seeking the soft mound of her breast and cupping it as if it were a flower.

'I want you, *anwylyd*,' he muttered huskily, his caressing hand discovering the ardency of her own response for himself. And then she heard him draw a quick sharp breath. Suddenly his encircling arm was a steel band, bruising her spine. Her eyes which she had closed while she abandoned herself to the pleasure of his caress, flew open in alarm.

'Your hair,' he said too evenly. 'What in the name of God have you done to your hair?'

She jerked herself upright, her hand flying guiltily upwards, but it was too late. The disguising headsquare had slipped off altogether. Gethyn bent and retrieved it from the floor of the car.

'So that was why,' he said, half to himself. He looked at her. His eyes still glowed, but it was anger, not passion, that lit them now. His lip curled contemptuously and she shrank. 'Why try to hide it?' he asked. 'When you've embarked on revenge, then you should have the courage of your convictions and see it through. Second thoughts can be dangerous, as you nearly discovered for yourself just then. You really had me fooled, you know. On the surface you're all woman, but there's nothing underneath—just a spiteful child. God, you must hate me!'

Something inside her was crying out, protesting that it had not been spite, only self-defence, but she knew she could not betray how completely she was in his power. Instead she let her own anger kindle from his.

'How dare you criticise me! My hair is my own and I'll do what I wish with it. I don't belong to you, Gethyn.'

'No?' His mouth twisted cynically. 'What did you have in mind at the wedding ceremony, may I ask? A short-term loan? Thanks, but I'm not interested.'

'You made that more than clear two years ago,' she whispered. 'Now drive me back to Plas Gwyn. I'm leaving. I won't even spend another night under your roof.'

'You think not?' The look he sent her as he set the car in motion again made her blench. 'Well, don't bank on it, my sweet wife, because I haven't finished with you yet, not by a long chalk. Perhaps I might just indulge in a little revenge on my own account.'

'I think you've already done so.' She tried to rally her fast-diminishing courage. 'I—I'm bitterly ashamed of what happened just now and . . .'

'Are you now?' he mocked savagely. 'And after only a few kisses too!'

'Oh, stop it, please!' She pressed her hands to her burning cheeks.

'I should practise that note of pleading,' he said. 'It's very effective, and you'll need it by the time I'm through with you.'

It was pointless trying to reason with him in this mood, she realised helplessly, and subsided back into her seat. The sun was blazing into the car, but she felt cold and chilled. She made herself think and plan for the moment when they arrived back at Plas Gwyn. Whatever he had in mind, once she was in the house, his aunt's presence should be some kind of protection for her. Her car keys were in her bag. It would be the work of minutes to throw the few things she had brought with her into her case. Her mind worked feverishly. Surely at some time she would be able to slip away from the house to her car? It wasn't feasible that Gethyn could watch every move she made.

She tried to force herself to be calm, to steady her racing pulses, to ignore the ache deep within her that spoke treacherously of fulfilment denied. Oh, God, what was he—some enchanter that he could hold her so easily in thrall? she asked herself helplessly. In that moment when he had murmured that he wanted her, she had been his for the taking. She would have gone with him willingly to whatever lonely eyrie he had chosen in these wild hills and gloried in the dark fierceness of his lovemaking.

But not now. Not since he had talked of spite and revenge. She put up her hand and touched the short tendrils of hair curving on to her face. Oh, she'd meant to make him angry, that was true, but that was only the half of it. It had been the partly joking, wholly sensual threat that he

had uttered before he left her to go shopping that morning that had driven her to do what she did. He'd spoken of
her hair across his pillow, aroused well-nigh unbearable
memories. It had seemed for a few mad moments that
by destroying her hair, she could in some way destroy his
power over her. She had never in her wildest dreams
imagined that he would react as he had done. There was
a brooding purpose about him as he sent the car rushing
smoothly along the narrow ribbon of road that frankly
terrified her.

And what a futile gesture it had been anyway. She had
cut her hair off to show Gethyn she was indifferent to him
and his desires, but a few brief minutes in his arms had
shown her very clearly that her sacrifice had been in vain.
The only refuge left to her now was flight.

Her hands clenched, her nails digging into her palms as
he turned the car into the track that led down to Plas Gwyn.
When they reached the parking spot under the trees, she
opened the passenger door herself and climbed out, without looking at him or speaking. She sent a single flickering
glance to reassure herself that her own car was still there,
remembering as she did so that she had over half a tank-
ful of petrol. That should be enough to get her well away
from here. She wouldn't take the direct route. It would be
too easy for him to follow her. She would set off in the
opposite direction—find some side roads to take her back
to the main thoroughfares and home.

She walked down the track towards the house, forcing
herself not to look back to see if he was following. It would
be a further humiliation to betray her concern about his
intentions. But he seemed in no hurry to pursue her and
she found she was quickening her own steps perceptibly as
she approached the house.

In the hall she encountered a flustered-looking Mrs Parry.

'Oh, you're back,' she exclaimed with evident relief.
'Every time Gethyn goes out, it's the same. That old phone
never stops ringing. There's someone hanging on for him
now. I thought I'd heard the car.'

'He won't be long.' Davina made herself speak normally.

but she was aware that Mrs Parry's eyes were on her rather searchingly as she went upstairs to her room. She seized her case and thrust her nightdress and toilet bag into it, then grabbed her black shawl from the back of a chair and piled it in on top of the other things. She was ready. She opened the door quietly and tiptoed along the landing until she reached the head of the stairs. Then she listened. Somewhere below she could hear Gethyn speaking and guessed by the pattern of the words that he was on the telephone. Silently she crossed her fingers in the fold of her skirt that it would be a long call, then she slipped quietly down, across the hall to the open front door and out again into the sunlight.

She ran up the track, stumbling in her haste, searching in her bag for the precious keys as she went. It seemed a lifetime before she reached the car and unlocked the door, listening all the time for the sounds of pursuit. But all was silence but for the distant sound of the sheep on the mountain. She slid into the driving seat and fitted the key into the ignition. The engine spluttered and died.

She bit her lip and waited for a minute. It was just cold, that was all, after standing for twenty-four hours. She needed more choke. She tried again. The car snorted feebly and was silent. She sat in the driving seat, twisting the key again and again, trying to will it to start, but it was hopeless. The battery must be flat, she thought. She groaned softly, crossing her arms on the steering wheel and resting her bowed head on them. Where, she wondered desperately, did she go from here?

She heard a sound outside the car and stiffened immediately, lifting her head to look around her, wary as a wild bird. Gethyn was standing a few feet away watching her through the windscreen with a faint, cold amusement. He walked round to her window and looked down at her.

'Having trouble?'

There was something in the way he said it that made her realise with impotent fury that whatever ailed the car it was not the battery. He had known exactly what was in her mind, and he'd done something to the engine. She couldn't begin to guess what it might be, because she was no mechanic, and he knew it.

'Go to hell,' she said quietly.

His teeth were very white, when he smiled, against his dark face.

'I've been there already,' he said very gently. 'Next time, *cariad*, I'll take you along.'

He strode over to his own car and got into the driving seat. The engine purred into instant life and as Davina watched, shaken and chagrined, he drove away up the track and disappeared.

CHAPTER SIX

It was the longest afternoon of Davina's life. After a fruit-less half-hour spent under the bonnet of the car, tentatively poking at various pieces of wiring, she decided fuming that she might as well give it up as a bad job and return to the house.

Her first act was to pick up the telephone and dial the local garage, but that didn't get her very far. A harassed male voice informed her that he had so much work on hand that he couldn't possibly get around to looking at her car for at least two days.

'Staying at Plas Gwyn, are you?' he added just before he rang off. 'Well, ask Gethyn Lloyd to have a look at it for you. He's not bad with motors, and it might be just a simple thing he could fix for you in a jiffy.'

Davina, seething as she replaced her own receiver, didn't doubt that for one minute!

Her next phone call was to her mother in London, but again fortune was not on her side. Mrs Greer was out.

Davina was beginning to feel quietly desperate as she walked into the sitting room and stood staring out of the window. It seemed that whether she liked it or not, she was stranded at Plas Gwyn for the time being. Her chances of hiring a car were remote in the extreme at this time of year, and she wasn't even sure where the nearest mainline station was.

She sighed, and folded her arms across her breasts, hugging herself tightly. Perhaps she was tending to over-react again, she told herself. She knew she had not mistaken the very real threat in Gethyn's words, but then she had made him angry so she had asked for trouble. On the other hand, she could not really believe that he would actually carry out any of the drastic action he had hinted at. When his temper cooled, he would surely see reason, she thought, and wished that she could feel more positive about it.

His behaviour to date could hardly be described as predictable, but then she had not behaved very sensibly either. She should never have come here in the first place, but having made the decision she should never have allowed Gethyn to get under her skin again in the way he had. And she should not have provoked him in turn. After all, she had come here to reach a civilised settlement with him, and now they were at each other's throats.

She put up a hand and rubbed the nape of her neck, missing the weight of her hair on it. She bitterly regretted that visit to the hairdressers' now, although she supposed in one way she should be glad she had gone. It was only his discovery of what she had done that had stopped Gethyn from making love to her, she thought miserably. She certainly hadn't tried to stop him, and that was something she would have to live with. She had no one but herself to blame. She had deliberately courted such a situation by allowing herself to be alone with him. There had always been this physical attraction between them, and she knew now that she ignored it at her peril.

Davina bit her lip. She was thankful Gethyn would never know that no one else had ever kissed or touched her like that. During the two years of their separation, she had never been even remotely tempted to go to bed with anyone else. She had retired behind a curtain of smiling aloofness which kept would-be admirers at a safe distance. Now it had been brought home to her with a vengeance that her defences were by no means impregnable.

She bowed her head. It was humiliating to have to acknowledge how readily she had responded to Gethyn, how willing she had been to satisfy his transient desire. She had not even paused to consider that there was now another woman in his life, and neither had he. She supposed unhappily that she should not have been too surprised by his conduct. His behaviour in America after they had parted had revealed just how lightly he regarded loyalty and fidelity in marriage. Rhiannon too might have a bitter lesson to learn one day, she thought, and for a moment she could almost feel pity for the girl.

'Oh, you're here, Davina.' Mrs Parry bustled into the room. 'Where's Gethyn gone? There's a list of messages for him and ...'

'I wouldn't know.' Davina interrupted the older woman more coldly than she had intended. 'I'm not his keeper.' She saw Mrs Parry's kind face take on a hurt expression and contrition overcame her. 'I'm sorry, Aunt Beth,' she apologised quickly. 'It's just that—where Gethyn goes and what he does—is really none of my business any more.' If it ever was, she added painfully under her breath.

Mrs Parry gave a quick frown. 'I don't understand the young people of today, I don't really,' she said fretfully. 'All this running in and out of marriage as if it didn't matter.'

Davina turned away. 'It takes two to make a bargain, Aunt Beth.' She kept her voice deliberately neutral. 'I think Gethyn probably prefers to be a free agent—for the time being at least,' she added, the thought of Rhiannon at the forefront of her mind. 'He finds the bonds of matrimony too tying.'

Mrs Parry snorted. 'What kind of nonsense is that?' she demanded. 'Why would he have saddled himself with a house like this if he wasn't thinking of settling down for good?'

'I don't know what his motives are,' Davina said a little wearily. 'But I can promise you that I don't figure in his future plans either here or anywhere else. And it's an arrangement that suits both of us. Please excuse me now. I'm going for a walk.'

She had no very clear idea of where she was going when she got outside the house. The sky had cleared miraculously, and the sun shone down on her unprotected head, awakening in her a longing for a cool breeze, and the sound of running water. She turned abruptly and set off through the deserted yard at the back of the house, making for the track which would lead up to the waterfall.

Little flies danced around her as she made her way up the rutted slope behind the house, and she slapped them away irritably with her hand. After she had been walking for about ten minutes, she paused and looked. Plas Gwyn nestled below her in the hollow, as secure and familiar in its untrammelled lines as a child's drawing. Mrs Parry had been right in one thing, she thought, sitting down on the short, springy turf and resting her back against a sunwarmed rock. It was the sort of house to settle down in. It seemed to breathe peace and comfort, a far cry from the university digs and cramped London flats that Gethyn had been used to. But would this kind of setting really bring him satisfaction. Judging by what he had said in response to her uncle's offer, he was quite prepared to set out on his travels again.

Her gaze wandered away from the house, tracing the track that led deeper into the valley below the dragon rock. She could just glimpse a cluster of grey stone and slate which she guessed must be the mill that Gethyn was renovating. That too was an enigma. It seemed incredible that a writer of his calibre could apparently turn his back completely on one part of his life in order to devote himself to a half-ruined woollen mill. Would he really find the answer to his creative urge in such comparatively mundane pursuits as weaving tweed for tourists? She shook her head in bewilderment. From her knowledge of Gethyn, it didn't seem possible that such a prosaic undertaking could fill his life to the exclusion of everything else. But then, she reminded herself, what did she really know of Gethyn?

She stood up abruptly and continued on her way up the steepening track towards the towering bulk of the mountain. The going was getting rougher all the time and the sandals she was wearing didn't help at all. The shoes she had bought in Dolgellau would have been ideal, but they, of course, were in Gethyn's car still. She bent and slipped off her sandals, and after a moment's hesitation took off her tights as well, tucking them into the pocket of her dress before continuing her walk, moving along the grass that bordered the path, relishing its coolness under her toes.

She could hear the sound of the waterfall long before it came into view. She rounded a corner, and saw that the path fell away suddenly down into a deep hollow, at the foot of which was the pool Mrs Fenton had mentioned. Above the pool, the water slid smoothly down over the dark rock, foaming gently over the boulders it encountered on its descent. Little waves lapped invitingly on the small beach of shingle and pebbles.

Davina needed no second invitation. She dropped her shoes in the shadow of a large rock and plunged down the slope towards the pool. She flinched momentarily as the cold water swirled round her ankles, but soon found the coolness refreshing after her walk. She scooped up a handful of water and trickled it over her wrists, enjoying the sensation on her warm flesh. She wished she had brought a swimsuit with her—the thought of a swim in this remote and peaceful spot had a potent appeal. She tilted her head back and stared up at the dragon rock. It had an austere grandeur all its own, she thought. A powerful presence, even.

She gave a wry smile, deriding herself for her own fancy. It was nonsense to imagine that a piece of stone, eroded by the elements, could have power of any kind, or to think that a bathe in the pool at the foot of the rock could possibly give her any kind of immunity against the all-too-human power that awaited her back at Plas Gwyn. All that a swim could do for her would be to make her feel cool and clean again, washing away the touch of his hands on her skin. She sighed bleakly, wishing that she could erase the memory of that delight from her mind as easily.

She stared around her, listening to the silence, registering the emptiness of the slope behind her, the utter solitariness of the place. There was absolutely no one about, she told herself. Who would see her if she did go for a swim? And the bra and briefs she was wearing were no more revealing than many bikinis seen on beaches these days. Her indecision at an end, she began to unfasten her dress. She folded it neatly and took it back to the rock where she had left her shoes, placing them on top of it to anchor it down.

This time as she entered the water, it merely felt welcomingly cool. She waded in until she was waist-deep, then

struck out strongly towards the waterfall. She swam round
in a long slow circle, keeping at a respectful distance. She
guessed that some underground channel must take the
water away and wanted to avoid any possible dangerous
currents. She floated on her back for a while, watching the
sky. High above a hawk hovered, its wings motionless
against the deep blue. Even in this peaceful place there were
predators, it seemed, and even as the thought came to her
she heard somewhere quite close at hand the rattle of a
pebble against someone's shoe. Tension filled her immediately. She turned in the water and swam quickly towards
the rocks at the other side of the pool. She was shivering
as she hauled herself out of the water and crouched among
the rocks. They afforded only the minimum of shelter. Anyone coming down the track to the pool would be almost
bound to spot her. She swallowed. There was no need to
panic, she told herself. Plenty of people must use these
hills—hikers, picnickers. Why jump to the conclusion that
the person coming along the track could only have one
identity? She was shivering now, and her teeth chattered.
Why on earth had she left her dress and sandals out in the
open, a plain advertisement of her presence? She could
only keep well down and rely on the intruder walking
straight past and over the mountain. She glanced down at
herself and gave an involuntary grimace. There was a
marked difference between the wisps of underclothing she
was wearing and a bikini, after all. Bikinis did not normally
become practically transparent in water.

She could hear no further sounds of approach and lifted
her head cautiously to look around. There was no one in
sight, yet a tingle of awareness told her that she was not
alone, that even at this moment someone might be standing at the top of the track, looking down into the hollow.
She ducked her head down again and looked around for a
more secure refuge. Timothy Fenton had said something
about a cave—the dragon's cave behind the waterfall. She
craned her neck. Was that a dark opening she could glimpse
behind the rush of the water? It was only a matter of yards

away, although getting to it would mean coming out into the open.

She kept very still for a moment, her ears pricked for the sound of footsteps or voices, but all was silent. So she stood up and began to edge her way very carefully across the rocks. It wasn't easy. The stones were slippery with water and slime and the spray from the waterfall felt like droplets of ice on her cooling skin.

She bit her lip. The cave seemed a definitely uninviting prospect, and she paused indecisively, staring across the pool at the track. She was just beginning to convince herself that the sharer of her solitude had gone on his way long before and that she was getting thoroughly chilled for nothing, when he came down the track towards the beach with his long easy stride.

A gasp broke from Davina's lips. Her instinct, it seemed, had been only too right. Any second now he would see her dress and sandals lying on the grass, she thought, and as if he was telepathic, she saw him pause and bend to pick them up.

She had never moved faster in her life. Her only thought was flight, and she dived for the cave, uncaring about the stones that stubbed at her toes and wrenched her ankle.

It wasn't really a cave at all—just a scooped-out space, dark, cold, running with moisture with barely enough room to stand up. Behind her a deep crack ran back into the mountain itself, but this wouldn't even admit the skinniest child. She leaned forward a little to see what Gethyn was doing, and wet fern fronds, clinging to a narrow ledge, brushed across her face. They smelt dank and cold, and she shivered again, miserably conscious that her exposed skin was covered in goosepimples. For a moment she found herself wishing that this was indeed a dragon's cave. A friendly, fire-breathing dragon would have been more than welcome right there and then. But no self-respecting mythical monster would have tolerated such a damp, cramped hideout even for five minutes. And she wasn't sure how much longer she would be able to last out either.

Her heart sank as she took another furtive peep across

the pool. She could see Gethyn quite clearly. He was sitting on a rock, smoking a cheroot, and her dress and sandals were lying on the ground at his feet. Fury rose in her. What kind of a cat-and-mouse game was this? For how long precisely did he intend to sit there while she froze to death in this miserable little hole? She rubbed her cold hands up and down her arms, to keep her circulation going.

How the hell had he known where to find her? she wondered despairingly. All she had said was that she was going for a walk, and yet he had traced her unerringly. He knew she was around because he had her clothes, yet for all he knew she might be drowned. He didn't show any signs of concern—of continuing his search, she thought, wrapping her arms across herself, and taking another cautious look.

At last he moved. He rose from his rock, pitched the half-smoked cheroot into the water, threw her dress across his shoulder and disappeared back the way he had come. Before his tall figure had vanished round the bend in the track, Davina was out of her hiding place. She was too numb and cold to swim. Instead she began a slow and painstaking traverse of the rocks before wading through comparatively shallow water to the beach.

She was thankful for the warmth of the sun on her body, but nothing could ease her inward chill. He had taken her dress—actually gone off with it. Her sandals too, of course, but that wasn't the disaster that her dress was. Barefoot, she could manage to get back to Plas Gwyn, but the mere idea of trying to make her way back down the mountainside next door to naked made her cringe.

Bastard! she raved inwardly. The fact that he had also crippled her car seemed relatively unimportant suddenly. Why, she might run into Huw Morgan—the returning pony-trekkers—anyone. She would have to wait here until her undies dried and gave her at least a semblance of decency, then try to brazen it out. After all, she had met no one on her way here. She would simply have to pray for similar good fortune on the return journey. Unless, of course, Gethyn had decided to organise some kind of reception committee for her, just to make her humiliation complete.

She sank down on the grass, a sudden feeling of weakness overpowering her. It was getting late, she thought, though she had no idea of the actual time because her watch was also in the pocket of her dress. An overwhelming urge to burst into tears was beginning to take possession of her, but she had to fight it. She couldn't let him win. Somehow she had to find the courage to make it look as if she was quite used to roaming about on remote Welsh hilltops wearing nothing but a few square inches of nylon fabric.

She put her arms round her knees and drew them up to her chin. I hate him, she told herself vehemently. I hate him! And at the realisation how far—how very far—that was from the truth, in spite of everything that had happened, she felt a harsh sob rise uncontrollably in her throat, and the tears she had tried vainly to suppress finally overcame her.

'Weeping for your damaged pride, lovely?'

Her head was up in an instant, her trembling lip firmly caught in her teeth at the sound of his sardonic voice. He hadn't gone far, she realised, just round the bend in the track. And there he had been waiting to see what she would do. Oh, why the hell had he had to find her crouched here on the ground, snivelling? Why couldn't she have marched up the path with her head in the air, whistling as if she didn't have a care in the world?

She glared at him. 'May I have my clothes, please?' she asked with icy calm.

'Must you?' His eyes went over her, insolently appraising, reminding her how totally inadequate her present covering was.

She got deliberately to her feet and returned his stare, fighting an urge to cover herself with her hands. 'Do tell me when you've seen enough,' she invited with dangerous politeness. 'I don't want to interfere with your voyeuristic little games, but I am getting rather cold.'

His smile was not pleasant. 'Then come here, *cariad*, and I'll warm you,' he suggested gently.

The silence that followed seemed endless. Davina heard herself swallow deafeningly. She stared down at the grass

at her feet, willing herself not to look at him—meet his
glance. Something compelling inside her was warning her
that would be fatal. There had been unholy amusement
dancing in the green eyes, and something else as well, less
easy to define, that could, if she wasn't careful, mesmerise
her across this few feet of turf into a situation that she
would regret for the rest of her life.

It was one thing to acknowledge deep inside herself that
all the old cravings were there, devastatingly rekindled. It
was quite another to betray herself to him any more than
she had done already. What had changed, after all? She
could still arouse his desire, but there was nothing new
about that. What she had to keep at the forefront of her
mind was the fact that his future plans had no place for
her at all. Besides, too much had happened between them
in the past. She could not let him use her for the casual
satisfaction of his physical appetites, which was how he
had regarded their marriage. He had not been prepared to
give her the shared companionship and responsibility—the
love that she had wanted more than anything else.

'What's the matter, lovely?' The caress in his words
tingled over her bare skin. 'Wishing that you'd stayed in
the dragon's cave and frozen to death?'

'Frankly, yes,' she replied shortly, her toes curling de-
fencelessly into the short-cropped grass.

She heard him laugh deep in his throat, and then he
tossed her dress towards her.

'Put it on,' he advised almost carelessly. 'Pneumonia
doesn't figure in my plans for you at all.'

Davina dragged the dress over her head, thrusting her
arms into the sleeves and working at the buttons with
fingers that shook as much from anger as from cold.

'Let's get one thing clear, shall we?' Her voice sounded
fierce. 'You have no plans for me, Gethyn. You forfeited that
right a long time ago. I came here to Wales for one reason
only, and you know it as well as I do: to persuade you to
divorce me now and not make us both wait for several more
years. That's what I intended, although I admit I may not
have gone the right way about it. But it's what I still want.'

'You've stated your case.' His tone was flat. 'Now do you want to hear what I want?'

'No.' She pressed her hands over her ears. 'No, I don't. I can't. If there's any mercy in you, Gethyn, stop tormenting me and let me go!'

'Mercy,' he said very evenly, 'was never further from my thoughts. I'll let you go, *cariad*, but in my own good time, and on my own terms. You talk about rights. What right had you to come here, asking me for favours? Did you really imagine all you'd have to do was smile and ask prettily and I'd fall in with everything you wanted?' He gave a derisive laugh. 'I suppose I should have known. That's been the story of your life up to now, hasn't it? Mummy's spoiled little girl, like a child in a toyshop, fancying everything she set eyes on and to hell with the consequences. Only sometimes the consequences are people, Davina, and they don't take kindly to being discarded when your fancy wanes. If I can teach you that much at least, perhaps this whole mess will have been worth it.'

'And perhaps not,' she said with a kind of quiet desperation. 'Gethyn, for God's sake, don't make everything worse. Don't leave us with even more to regret.'

He shook his head mockingly. 'I shall have nothing to regret, *cariad*.'

'Not even the hurt you're going to do to the girl you're going to marry?' She stared at him entreatingly. 'She doesn't want me here now. If she were to suspect even for a moment that the relationship between us had—altered in any way . . .' She lifted her shoulders in a helpless shrug. 'I can't believe you want that to happen.'

'Perhaps not,' he said softly. 'But it's something I'll have to risk.'

'Oh, God,' she whispered. 'It's true, isn't it? You don't care, do you? All that matters is your damaged pride, and the gratification of your instincts. You've said some hard things to me, Gethyn. I may have deserved some of them— I don't know. But are you really any better? You're incapable of normal human decency. You—you're an animal!'

'Am I now?' He was smiling, but his voice was taut with

anger. 'Well, that seemed to suit you well enough once upon a time. I don't remember you complaining about my animal-like behaviour before I married you. In fact quite the reverse. Until something or someone reminded you that you were a respectable middle-class virgin, and that desire was a dirty word. And then the ice formed.' His mouth twisted. 'But it melted before, Davina, and it can again. Who knows? The man who follows me into your bed may even have cause to thank me.'

She cried out and her hand came up to strike him full across his dark, jeering face, but he read her intention and his fingers gripped her wrist like a vice before she could make contact. At the same time, he gave her arm a brutal jerk so that she stumbled forward, half falling against him. His eyes glinted down into her white face.

'If you want to play rough, Davina, I'll be happy to accommodate you, but don't complain if you're the one who ends up bruised.'

He released her almost contemptuously and stood aside to allow her to precede him up the track. Her legs were shaking under her, but she managed the ascent somehow, very conscious that he was following her. At the top he halted her, his hand on her arm. His teeth gleamed in a sardonic smile.

'I imagine you can find your own way back to Plas Gwyn. I'll see you there later. Oh, and by the way'—as she turned dully away—'don't duck and hide, Davina. We're on my territory now, and I happen to know all the hiding places.'

She collected the shreds of her dignity remaining to her and set off towards the house. Her willpower faltered at one point and she could not resist a swift glance back over her shoulder to see if he was watching her go, but the hillside behind her was empty. Only the shadow of the great dragon rock remained, stretching out in the late afternoon sun to cross her path, as if in silent warning.

She felt unutterably weary when she reached the house. She was thankful Mrs Parry was not hovering to oversee her return, and hurried across the hall, intending to make for the stairs and the comparative safety of her room. But as she got to the stairs, Huw Morgan emerged from the back of the house carrying a large flat basket piled high with logs. His brows rose when he saw Davina.

'Still with us, then, *bach*? That's good news.'

'I'm glad you think so.' She couldn't keep the bite out of her voice, and he gave an exaggerated wince.

'Someone would seem to have upset you,' he remarked. 'I won't enquire further.' His gaze sharpened. 'What have you done to your hair?'

'Had it cut,' she snapped. 'Any objection?'

'Oh, so that's it,' he observed meditatively. He shook his head rather sadly. 'No, Gethyn wouldn't like that. He wouldn't like it at all.'

'No, he doesn't.' A sudden inspiration had seized her, and she made herself smile at him, albeit ruefully. 'I—I'm *persona non grata* round here at the moment, and I think the best thing I can do is make a tactful withdrawal—only . . .' She hesitated.

'Only what?' he prompted.

'So silly.' She spread out her hands ingenuously. 'There's something a teeny bit wrong with the car. It simply wouldn't start earlier, and things being as they are, I can hardly ask Gethyn to fix it for me. I don't suppose you . . .' She let the words drift away invitingly.

Huw pursed his lips reluctantly. 'Well, I'm no mechanic, but if it's only a simple thing, I daresay I could manage it. I'll just put these in the sitting room for Mrs Parry and then I'll be with you.'

Davina could not help a sneaking feeling of triumph as he accompanied her up to the parking space. By the time Gethyn returned she could be away and gone. She watched while he tried to start the engine, but unavailingly. He was frowning as he got out and raised the bonnet.

'Sure your battery isn't flat, Davina?'

'I don't think so,' she said honestly. 'I—I think it's far more likely to be some slight mechanical fault.'

He gave an uninformative grunt as he bent over the engine. Eventually he straightened and shot her a peculiar look. 'Odd kind of fault,' he remarked. 'Your rotor arm is missing.'

Davina swallowed. 'Is that serious?'

'Well, the car won't start without it,' he returned.

She tried to smile again. 'I wonder what's happened to it?'

'I wonder too.' He gave her a long look. 'You may be *persona non grata, bach*, but someone wants you to stay around. Sure you haven't been feeding me a line?'

'Why should I want to do that?' she protested weakly.

He made no reply, but slammed down the bonnet with an air of finality.

She tried again. 'Is there no way, Huw, that you could just—fix it up for me, even temporarily, until I can get to a garage?'

'No, Davina. Removing the rotor arm is one of the most effective ways there are of disabling a car. Da learned to do it during the war when he was in the R.A.F. It stopped people joyriding on your petrol, he said.'

There was nothing more to be said. She trailed embarrassedly beside him back to the house, only thankful that he was not asking any probing questions. In the hall, she detained him.

'I suppose you wouldn't give me a lift to the nearest railway station?' she asked, not troubling to conceal the pleading note in her voice.

'You suppose right.' Huw raised his eyebrows. 'Don't look so stricken, *bach*. It's one of my rules—never interfere between husband and wife, and I've already broken it once where you and Gethyn are concerned.'

'Yes,' she said quietly. She wondered whether Huw had been made to suffer any repercussions for taking her out that night. It would not really be fair to expose him to Gethyn's wrath for a second time. Besides, Huw had problems of his own. She asked herself if he was aware just how serious the relationship was between Gethyn and Rhiannon, but she could not bring herself to ask him outright. If he did know, it would explain his reluctance to help her get away from Plas Gwyn. He must be hoping that she would be the wedge to drive Gethyn and Rhiannon apart.

Huw was watching her. 'Mrs Parry has some tea on the go if you'd like some.'

'No, thanks. I'm not thirsty.' It wasn't true. She could have drained a reservoir, but she couldn't face the homely kitchen, and Mrs Parry's inquisitorial gaze over the tea-cups.

She closed the bedroom door behind her and leaned against it for a moment, her eyes closed. The first thing she saw when she opened them was that the bed was littered with parcels. Gethyn, it seemed, had been up to her room—his room, she remembered bitterly. She eyed her morning's purchases with dislike. She'd never particularly wanted to see any of them again, but at least they would be a change from her shirtwaister, which had stood up gallantly to the rough treatment it had received, but was now looking thoroughly dejected. She glanced at herself in the mirror. In spite of its wilted state, the dress still conveyed an air of appealing femininity which she was far from anxious to emphasise just now. Jeans and a sweater would be far more appropriate for the current state of her emotions.

She selected a handful of clothing more or less at random, and went off to the bathroom. There was a heavy bolt on the inside of this door, and she felt infinitely more secure once it was thrust into place. As she ran the water into the bath, she kept eyeing the bolt and wondering how long it would take a really determined man to break down the door, but at the same time she knew there was no way she was going to find out. Gethyn, she was sure, would emerge the winner from any encounter she cared to stage, and she shrank from the thought of making an ugly scene in front of a houseful of strangers.

She lay for a long time in the hot water, hoping that it would have the usual therapeutic effect of relaxing some of the tensions out of her body. But not this time. She was still wincingly, nerve-bitingly on edge as she stepped out on to the small bath mat and began to dry herself on the rather rough towel.

When she was dressed again, she had to admit she was not wholly dissatisfied with her appearance. The new haircut and the close-fitting dark clothes made her look very young and emphasised the delicacy of her bone structure. Normally she would have added gloss to her lips and a touch of blusher to her pale cheeks, but not tonight. This time she was aiming for the well-scrubbed, rather boyish look, she thought ruefully—a ploy of desperation if ever there was one!

The pony-trekkers had returned, she knew. While she was bathing and dressing, she had heard various pairs of feet ascending the stairs and the sound of laughter and voices. So it was no surprise when she entered the kitchen a little later to find Rhiannon sitting at the table. She glanced up at Davina's entrance, and her brows drew together.

'Good God,' she remarked unflatteringly. 'What have you done to yourself?'

Davina sighed. 'I've changed my image a little,' she returned equably. 'I should have thought you'd be pleased. You didn't seem to care for the previous one very much.'

Rhiannon shrugged rudely. 'I don't give a damn what you look like,' she retorted. 'It's your presence I object to, not your physical appearance. Does this mean you're staying on?'

Davina was forced to smile unwillingly at the overt note of disgust in the other girl's voice.

'I'm afraid so,' she acquiesced, sitting down at the table. 'At least until my car is mended.'

'What's the matter with it?' Rhiannon sat up. 'Huw knows a bit about cars. He was around here earlier. I'll get him to have a look at it, if you want.'

'He already did.' Davina held up a detaining hand. 'But I'm afraid it's no use. Some vital part seems to have vanished.'

'Oh, has it now?' Rhiannon said aggressively. 'And I suppose you think you've been very clever.'

'Don't be a fool!' Davina's eyes widened impatiently. 'I didn't do it. As a matter of fact, I'm more keen to get away

from here than you are to see me go. In fact'—she leaned
forward making no attempt to disguise her eagerness—'you
could help me, Rhiannon.'

'Why should I want to do that?' Rhiannon was frankly
sceptical.

'Because I won't be able to leave here until you do. You
can drive, can't you? You could take me to the nearest
station.'

Rhiannon hesitated. 'I can drive—yes.'

'Then will you do it?'

There was a long pause. Davina's hands clenched into
nervous fists at her side as she waited impatiently for the
other girl's answer. Eventually Rhiannon looked up, and
Davina saw with a sinking heart that there had been no
lessening of the hostility in her gaze.

'No, I won't,' she said. 'You must think I'm the complete
country bumpkin, Miss Clever-from-London. Do you think I
don't know what you're up to? Not making much headway
at the moment, are you, no matter what you do, so you
think you'll do better back on your own territory. You think
that if you take off, Gethyn will come after you. You want
to get him away from Plas Gwyn—away from me. Well, it
won't work!'

Davina groaned inwardly. Rhiannon, she thought wryly,
gave her the credit for being much more devious than she
actually was.

'You're utterly wrong,' she said quietly. 'Believe me, it
will cause far less heartache for everyone if I just—go. No
one need ever know you helped me.'

'Well, I don't think I'm wrong.' Rhiannon pushed back
her chair and stood up. 'And I've no intention of helping
you. Oh, why did you have to come here?' she added in a
savage undertone. 'He would have forgotten all about you,
if only you'd stayed away.'

Davina bent her head. 'You can't regret my visit any more
than I do myself,' she said. But Rhiannon was plainly not
listening and presently Davina heard the slam of the back
door behind her.

She sighed and stared around her. She had never felt

more at a loss in her life. She tried to tell herself that
Gethyn's threats were simply an attempt to punish her—as
if she'd not been punished enough, she thought despairingly—and that having given her a severe fright, he would
let her go. But the argument was unconvincing to say the
least. There had been something implacable about him that
suggested only too strongly that he had meant every word.

She shuddered convulsively. The pitiable thing was that
what he had said was true. Her—ice, for want of a better
word, had melted for him in the past, and she had little
doubt, looking back bitterly to her almost fevered response
to him only that morning, that he would have little difficulty in seducing her to urgent surrender if he chose to do
so. She was ashamed to admit it, yet it was the truth.
Pride might tell her that she could not allow herself to be
taken on such terms, but an older emotion than pride murmured that she might have very little choice in the matter.

Suddenly the kitchen seemed oppressively warm and she
pulled at the neck of her sweater. She went to the back
door and opened it, hesitating for a moment. She did not
want another confrontation with Rhiannon, but the other
girl was nowhere in sight. In fact, the yard seemed deserted. Even Huw Morgan seemed to have vanished, the
only sign that he was still around being his Landrover
which was parked in the middle of the yard. Davina gave it
an irritable glance as she wandered past. Huw also had an
unexpectedly stubborn streak under his easy-going exterior,
but in fairness she could understand his motives in wanting
her to stay around. If she was to be reconciled with Gethyn,
then he would be able to step in to console Rhiannon. It
was all so simple viewed from his angle. Davina began to
feel like a helpless pawn in a chess game—a thing to be
used for the furtherance of a deeper aim, and then sacri-
ficed when it was of no further use.

Her temper rose at the thought. What was she doing,
allowing them all to manipulate her like this? For heaven's
sake, she had come here with one aim in view, backed up
by the secure life she had created for herself. Now, in a

matter of hours, she had degenerated into a quivering mass of doubts and fears and inconsistencies as if she had no life—no personality of her own. And all because of a man on whom she had already wasted too many tears.

She wasn't a helpless child. She was a woman. All right, so she'd got herself into a mess, but there was no law which said she had just to wait demurely for retribution to catch up with her.

She swung round and gave Huw's Landrover another long, hard look. Then she walked round it and looked into the back. It was not an inviting proposition. The hard floor was coated with what she devoutly hoped was mud, and in addition there was a haphazard jumble of boxes, a coil of rope, two half-filled sacks and what appeared to be a tarpaulin sheet. Whatever it was, it was big—quite big enough to cover anyone who might take it into her head to climb into the back and wait for Huw to drive away.

She glanced warily about her, but the yard was still deserted. The main difficulty was that she had no idea when Huw was planning to leave. It was still broad daylight and would remain so for several hours. Could she hope to remain unnoticed without the shelter of friendly darkness? She would have to hope that Huw would simply get in and drive away without checking the rear of the vehicle. Once they got to the farm, she was sure that Mrs Morgan would help her, if she appealed to her sympathy.

She wouldn't bother taking her suitcase or any of the clothes she had brought with her, she decided. They could just be abandoned, but she would need her briefcase and her handbag. She bit her lip. She could not risk disappearing too soon, or Gethyn would start searching for her, but she would fetch her things and stow them under the tarpaulin. All she would have to do then was keep a watchful eye on Huw and gauge when he was ready to take his departure.

She hurried back through the kitchen and up to her room. She took out the papers relevant to Gethyn's American trip and stuffed them into the top drawer of the dressing chest. He could find them there when she had gone, she told herself. Uncle Phil would understand why she had been unable to bring back a definite answer.

She looked round the room with a smile of satisfaction as she stood at the door. It still looked thoroughly occupied, and her nightgown draped across the bed was a really convincing touch, she decided. Her luck held as she went downstairs. Mrs Parry was standing in the sitting room, her back towards the door, chatting to the Fentons, and she did not turn as Davina wandered past with deceptive casualness, her briefcase concealed rather awkwardly behind her back. She raced across the deserted kitchen and peeped into the yard. The Landrover still stood there, and it was the work of a minute to drop her bag and briefcase into the back of it, and drag the tarpaulin sheet to cover it. It smelled musty as she tugged at it, and her lip curled at the thought of having to get underneath it. It was ludicrous that she had to go to these lengths, she told herself defiantly, and another item to add to the score she had to settle with Gethyn.

When Mrs Parry came into the kitchen she was sitting at the table glancing through the local paper, which she had found lying on a chair. Fortunately, her hostess was too busy for more than a perfunctory question about her day, and whether she had enjoyed her walk. Davina answered casually and Mrs Parry seemed quite satisfied with this.

The next hour or so was a scramble to serve the evening meal to the visitors in the dining room. Rhiannon appeared to act as the waitress as usual, and Davina was left to lay the kitchen table for the family's own meal. To her secret satisfaction, Mrs Parry called to her to set an extra place as Huw would be eating with them. If he stayed at Plas Gwyn until it was dark, it would make things much easier, she thought, her spirits rising.

The meal that evening was turkey with forcemeat stuffing and all the trimmings, followed by an apple charlotte with thick cream. In spite of her nervousness, Davina found that a day spent almost totally in the fresh air had sharpened her appetite and she did full justice to the meal, in spite of the fact that Gethyn had appeared just as they were sitting down and had stationed himself opposite to her.

To her fury she had felt a tinge of colour stain her cheeks as he pulled out his chair and sat down with a murmured apology to his aunt for his lateness. His own face gave nothing away, she thought, studying him covertly under her lashes as he talked to Huw. But there was an air of certainty about him tonight that galled her almost unbearably. It gave her immense satisfaction to imagine his feelings when he realised she had eluded him after all.

For a moment she wondered what she would do if he took the course of action that Rhiannon had suggested and pursued her to London, but she told herself she had little to fear. In London, she had her family to protect her. Besides, she thought he would be reluctant to give anyone the impression that her actions were important to him. Because they were not, as she knew to her cost. After all, when she had written to him that last time to tell him their marriage was over, he had made no move to get her to change her mind, or even to attempt to see her again to talk things over. He had been happy to accept her decision then. Perhaps common sense would prevail with him yet again once her escape was a *fait accompli*. And he had Rhiannon to console him, after all.

It was frightening how desolate that realisation made her feel. If only he had once given some sign that he cared for her, how different things might have been between them. But he cared for no one and nothing but himself. She had learned that the hard way, and Rhiannon would have to accept the same lesson.

'Penny for them, Davina.' Huw leaned across the table towards her as Mrs Parry placed cups of her strong powerful coffee brew before them. 'You look a bit lost, *bach*. Why don't we all go out for a drink tonight?' He turned to Gethyn. 'Must keep her entertained, or she may go skipping off back to London.'

For a horrified moment, Davina thought he was about to spill the beans about her request for help earlier. Panic forced her into speech. She even managed a smile.

'Oh, I don't think there's much chance of that.' She deliberately didn't look at Gethyn. 'Life—life has become much too interesting just lately.'

And let him make what he likes of that, she thought. No doubt his vanity would tell him that she was looking forward to bedtime with eager anticipation. Well, he would soon learn his mistake.

'Well, how about it?' Huw persisted. 'Do you fancy going out tonight?'

'Count me out,' Rhiannon said immediately, spooning sugar into her coffee.

'Another time, maybe, Huw.' Gethyn leaned back in his chair, and Davina was acutely aware that he was watching her intently. 'It's been a long day and an early night wouldn't come amiss.'

The direction of his gaze and the overt note of lazy amusement in his voice could have left no one around the table in any doubt of his intentions, Davina realised furiously. She could see Mrs Parry looking faintly surprised, but gratified nonetheless.

'Oh well, if that's the way of it,' Huw grinned. 'Sure you won't change your mind, Rhiannon?'

'Quite sure.' Rhiannon's chair scraped deafeningly across the floor as she got up, a bright spot of colour in either cheek. Davina felt real compassion for the girl. She looked totally stunned. She saw Huw's hand go out to her for a second, then fall to his side as if he recognised that this was not the moment.

She knew a moment's anxiety as she wondered whether he would decide the tactful thing would be to take his leave. There was no way she could get out of the kitchen and into the back of the Landrover without everyone being quite well aware what she was up to, and she could hardly follow him out on some pretext either. Thanks to Gethyn, she was suddenly the centre of some rather unwelcome attention. He had done it deliberately, of course, prompted by her own comment about her reluctance to leave.

She drank the rest of her coffee very slowly, trying to appear unconcerned. Perhaps he was really convinced that

she had meant it, that she was willing to resume an intimate relationship with him on any terms. Or was he simply
trying to goad her into another piece of self-betrayal? Well,
this time it just wouldn't work!

When her coffee was finished, she excused herself quietly
and left the room. She wandered through the hall, glancing
into the sitting room on her way and exchanging smiling
greetings with the Fentons, and refusing Timothy's eager
offer of a game of Ludo.

'I've eaten too big a meal,' she said, patting her stomach
ruefully. 'I think I ought to take a stroll and work some of
it off.'

Tim accompanied her to the front door. It was clear he
was only waiting for the slightest hint of an invitation, and
he would have accompanied her, and she felt mean at deny-
ing him. He was a nice kid, and the Fentons were going
home tomorrow. As she would be herself, she was forced to
remind herself.

'Have you walked up to the waterfall yet, Mrs Lloyd?' he
asked rather wistfully. And when she nodded, 'Did you find
the cave—and the dragon?'

Davina smiled. 'The cave, certainly, but the dragon
seemed to be out.'

'Do you think he exists?' Tim's eyes were fixed eagerly
on her face. 'You don't think it's just the wind blowing
through a crack in the rock like Huw Morgan says, do you?'

'No,' she said, her thoughts flicking back to the events
of the afternoon, the menacing shadow that had seemed to
follow her as she fled from Gethyn's anger. 'He's there all
right.'

Tim gave a blissful sigh, and she smiled down at him,
imagining the tales he would tell when he got back to
school of the dragon that still crouched inside its lonely
mountain.

She pushed her hands into the pockets of her jeans and
strolled down the path towards the gate. The goat pricked
up her ears as she went past, and Davina gave her a brief
scratch on the head, maintaining a wary distance in case

Arabella decided that her sweater was preferable as a diet to grass.

She paused at the gate as if making up her mind which direction to take and then turned very casually and began to walk round the house. She paused in the shadow of one of the outbuildings and looked across the yard. She could see Mrs Parry in the scullery, but her head was bent and she was oblivious to anything that might be taking place outside as she concentrated on the washing up, so Davina seized her chance. She was across the yard like lightning and swung herself with little effort into the back of the Landrover. She resolutely closed her nostrils to the multifarious odours that assailed them and crouched down. There were a few empty sacks as well, that were dry and not too dirty, although she had her suspicions about their previous contents. But she could not afford to be too choosy, she told herself, arranging them on the floor under the tarpaulin, and then crawling under it herself.

She had no idea how long she remained there in the noisome darkness which managed in some strange way to be both chilly and stifling at the same time. She only knew she was on the point of admitting defeat and going back to the house when dimly in the distance she heard the back door opening and the sound of voices approaching. Her heart sank and she tensed instinctively as she recognised Gethyn's resonant, drawling tones. Oh, why did it have to be him of all people come to see Huw off the premises? She strained her ears trying to hear what they were saying, but it was impossible. She made herself as small as possible under the sheltering tarpaulin and held her breath. Even so when something bulky descended on top of her with considerable force she was hard put to it not to cry out in alarm. At least it was nothing human, she tried to console herself ruefully as she tried to cope with this new discomfort.

She heard Huw give a quick shout of laughter, then the vehicle rocked as he climbed into the driving seat. She lay very still, every nerve stretched to screaming point, waiting for the engine to start. When at last they began to move

forward amid shouted goodnights, she could have wept
with relief. For good or ill, she was on her way, and she
would never see Gethyn again. Pain that had nothing to do
with cold or cramp lashed at her, and she crushed it down
relentlessly. She had to forget about him now. Anything else
was utterly unthinkable. There was no future for them, and
there never had been, and that was a fact she should have
learned by now. Certainly he had had no compunction in
teaching it to her. She could not exist merely to satisfy a
transient fancy.

The next few minutes were pure anguish as the Landrover jolted its way up the track. Davina felt as if every
bone in her body was breaking. She closed her eyes and bit
her lip hard as the wheels went over every new rut and pot-
hole. And it seemed to go on for ever. Surely they would
be at the road soon? She would liked to have taken a
cautious peep out, but did not dare. If Huw found her before they arrived at the Morgans' farm, he might feel it
incumbent on him to drive her back to Plas Gwyn.

She was almost at screaming point when the Landrover
suddenly stopped. For a moment she stretched herself involuntarily, then froze. They hadn't reached the road yet;
she knew they hadn't. So why had they stopped? Had Huw
divined somehow that she was there? Or more prosaically,
but even more disastrously, had this blighted vehicle simply
given up the ghost in some way?

She shrank as she realised Huw was getting out of the
driver's seat. She heard stones and pebbles clatter as he
walked round the Landrover to the back. She made herself
keep perfectly still as the bulky weight, whatever it had
been, was hauled off her, and she heard his footsteps reced-
ing.

She waited for a few moments, then very cautiously
pushed the tarpaulin off and looked around her. She realised
incredulously that she must have been crouched in the back
for several hours, because it was now twilight. The Landrover was parked in front of a building of some sort. The
door stood open and lamplight was flooding out reassuringly. Davina got painfully on to her knees and gave the

house a closer look. It wasn't a very large place. She had
imagined the Morgans' farmhouse would be considerably
more opulent, but as her eyes accustomed themselves to the
new light, she could see that another much larger building
stood nearby, and somewhere, close at hand, she could
hear the sound of running water.

One thing was certain. She could not endure another
moment under that tarpaulin, and when she saw Huw and
the inevitable recriminations were over, she would suggest
acidly that he cleaned his Landrover out occasionally. She
got stiffly down, brushing dirt and creases from her clothes,
then walked towards the welcoming lamplight. Somewhere
to sit down, she thought longingly, that did not bump or
lurch, threatening to dislocate your spinal column. And a
warm drink. Even if the Morgans were not very pleased to
see her, surely they wouldn't deny her that much at least.
She hesitated, then walked resolutely through the low doorway.

It wasn't a large room, furnished at random, it seemed
from a variety of junk shops. The lamp stood in the centre
of a solid old-fashioned table, and beyond it a wood fire
flickered and crackled on a stone hearth, making the room
dance unnervingly with shadows.

Davina stood looking round her, utterly disconcerted,
then one of the shadows detached itself and came forward
into the lamplight and her next breath caught in her throat.

'Alone at last, Davina,' Gethyn said quite gently, and
walked past her to kick the door shut, closing them in together into this intimacy of soft flickering light with heart-
thudding finality.

CHAPTER SEVEN

HE turned and leaned back against the door, his arms folded across his chest, as if to emphasise that her line of retreat was cut off. His green eyes seemed to taunt her as they began a lingering head-to-toe assessment that made her feel hot all over.

'I did warn you that you might end up bruised, *cariad*, though this wasn't altogether what I had in mind,' he said at last.

'Where's Huw?' she demanded huskily.

He lifted a lazy shoulder. 'Back at Plas Gwyn, I suppose, lending Rhiannon his shoulder to cry on.'

'You're quite heartless, aren't you?' she said hotly. 'Don't you care about the hurt you've caused that poor child?'

His eyes gleamed appreciatively. 'That "poor child" is very little younger than you are. And it was inevitable that she was going to be hurt sooner or later. Besides, she has Huw to pick up the pieces. I wouldn't be surprised if this wasn't a turning point for them.'

'And you don't even care.'

He shrugged again. 'It's very flattering to be given such wholehearted devotion, but I always knew I could never live up to Rhiannon's god-like image of me. Huw's ideal for her, and maybe she'll get round to realising it now.'

'But you were going to marry her.'

He shook his head. 'I'm married to you, Davina. A fact I've never forgotten for a minute, even if you have.'

She flung up her head. 'I don't know how you have the gall to say such a thing,' she said, her voice shaking with anger.

'Because it happens to be the truth.' Anger stirred in his own even tones. '*Duw*, Davina, haven't I made it clear enough in the past few days? I'm damned if I'll just agree

141

to a divorce and wave you goodbye. I want you, and this time I intend to keep you.'

'Against my will?' she asked between her teeth.

He smiled sardonically. 'Tell me that in the morning,' he suggested, and came away from the door with a purpose about him that set her pulses pounding. She backed away from him, until the table brought her up short. Her gaze went all over the room looking for a way out. But there was none. In the corner, a flight of rather ramshackle wooden steps led up to the upper storey—but that was the last direction she wanted to take, she thought, biting at her lower lip until the blood came.

He halted barely a foot away from her and his eyes were quizzical as they studied her pale face.

'And now what?' he inquired interestedly. 'Shall we continue this chase round the room, or shall we sit by the fire in a civilised manner and drink coffee together? I imagine you could do with some after that bone-shaking ride of yours.'

She would have liked to have flung the offer haughtily back in his face, but common sense prevailed, and she nodded awkwardly.

'Go and sit down,' he ordered, giving her a not ungentle push towards the fire. 'It's only a wooden rocking chair, I'm afraid, but there are a couple of pillows in the pack over there. You can use those if you like.'

So that was what he had thrown on top of her, she thought, as she knelt beside the large bundle and began to unfasten the strap that held it securely. Not just pillows either, she found, but sheets and blankets and a quilt. Her face flamed as the implications of this came home to her. No doubt presently Gethyn would expect her to help him to make up their marriage bed. Well, she would see him in hell first! She rescued a pillow and carried it over to the elderly rocking chair by the fire. Gethyn was busy at a small calor gas stove in one corner of the room.

She settled herself in the chair, wincing slightly.

'What is this place?'

'Well, it isn't the Morgans' farm.' He sent her a satirical

glance over his shoulder. 'I presume that's where you thought you were bound.'

'Yes,' she admitted. There was little point in trying to deny it. Gethyn seemed to have been one step ahead of her all the time. 'How—how did you know I was in the back?'

'Intuition,' he said mockingly. 'It seemed the logical step for you to take, especially after Huw had told me about your fruitless appeal to his chivalry earlier on.' He smiled. 'We simply agreed to swop vehicles for the evening, that's all. Although I did check you were actually in the back before I drove off. Your fetching shape was quite unmistakable even underneath a tarpaulin. Besides, a corner of your hand-bag was poking out.'

'If I'd known——' she said unsteadily.

'Oh, you don't have to describe what your reaction would have been.' He raised a laconic hand. 'You've already made that more than clear. But I'm simply doing you a favour, if you did but know it. You did say that you weren't prepared to spend another night at Plas Gwyn. Now, you don't have to.'

He poured the coffee into two battered tin mugs and carried them across the room, offering her one which she accepted with a perfunctory murmur of thanks. Her brain seemed to be going round in endless circles. She couldn't really believe what was happening to her. She presumed that her present surroundings were part of the old mill that Gethyn was renovating. Judging by the rudimentary furnishings, he also camped there periodically. A shiver ran through her, and she inched her chair fractionally nearer to the blazing logs, although she was perfectly aware that it had not been a purely physical reaction. In fact, it was very warm in the small room, and the fire had obviously been started some hours before. Everything in readiness, she thought, clasping her hands round the warmth of the mug, and herself walking blithely into the trap of her own devising.

Suddenly events seemed to be taking on a previously unguessed-at pattern, as if the bait had been laid months before when Gethyn had refused to answer Mr Bristow's letters, knowing, perhaps, that she would come to find out his reasons for herself. And she, all too predictably, had done precisely that.

But, if her reasoning was correct, why had he done all this? It was all very well for him to claim that she was still his wife and arrogantly demand the resumption of their marital relationship, but he had been the one who had walked out. For two years—nothing. Not a word, not a sign, yet now this. As if she was some plaything to be picked up and discarded at will!

That was what hurt, of course. That and the realisation of how much she had given away in her blind, seeking response to his lovemaking only hours before. What, after all, did he care about her mind and her heart, as long as her body wanted him?

It was almost a shock to raise her eyes and find that he was looking at her, and that there was something in his regard which told her plainly he had been watching her for quite a while and had probably had little difficulty in reading the various emotions which had occupied her mobile face. It was quite bad enough to know that presently he would no doubt insist on stripping her physically naked. It was too much to know that he was attempting much the same thing to her mental processes.

'What are you trying to prove?' She made her voice as even as possible.

'A good question.' His voice was mocking. 'But surely there should be no question of proof between husband and wife. Shouldn't—most things be taken on trust?'

'I think it's a little late for that, don't you?' She took a sip at the hot coffee. It seemed to put heart into her.

'If I thought that, *cariad*, then we should not be here. And you question far too much, as well. That was what was wrong from the beginning. You suddenly started to ask yourself just what you were doing getting into bed with this wild Welsh savage. After all, you didn't even know if I was housetrained. I'm not objecting to the questions in themselves, you understand. You're as entitled to have last-minute doubts as the next one. It was just the timing of them that I found unfortunate.'

His tone was light, and she tried to reply in the same spirit.

'I suppose the start of the honeymoon is a little late to ask questions—but it needn't have made a great deal of difference—if I'd got the answers I wanted. As it was . . .' She tried a casual shrug.

'As it was,' he said without emotion, 'it never occurred to you, my sweet egotist, that I might have had some doubts myself as to what I was taking on, and that the answers I came up with were equally unsatisfactory. I wondered, you see, if the realisation that you'd actually married a man and not merely a success might be too bitter a pill for you to swallow. And how right I turned out to be. But Mummy had brainwashed you well, hadn't she, lovely? You could only think of yourself in terms of being an asset. It never occurred to you that you could be a liability.'

The tin mug and the remains of the coffee crashed unheeded to the floor as Davina leapt out of her chair.

'You bastard!' Her voice shook uncontrollably. 'You dare to reproach me—you dare . . .'

'I dare a great deal, Davina, as you will shortly find out.' He kicked away the upturned packing case he had been lounging on before her outburst, and took one long stride towards her.

'No!' She tried to back away, but the rocking chair was in the way, catching the back of her legs making her stumble. 'No—you ran out on me.'

He laughed unpleasantly. 'That's rich, coming from you, Davina. You've been running all your life.' His voice roughened, took on a note that chilled her. 'Why, you even ran away from motherhood. Or were you hoping I might have conveniently overlooked that most salient point? You owe me that child, Davina. And if by some good fortune you should conceive tonight, then I'll keep you chained to my wrist for the next nine months. You won't cheat me again.'

She cried out at that, her hands pressed tremblingly to

her stricken face. Tears were scalding at the back of her eyes and hurting her throat.

'You—you can't say that,' she choked. 'You don't know —you can't imagine what I went through . . .'

'I have a pretty fair idea.' His face in the firelight looked diabolic. 'I think it was only the knowledge that you'd suffered that stopped me from coming back to Britain and half-killing you.'

'Oh, God,' she was crying openly now, the tears spilling endlessly down her white cheeks. 'How can you be so cruel?'

'Cruelty, is it?' His voice was harshly mocking. He seemed totally impervious to her distress. 'Perhaps you imagine you have a monopoly?' His hand gripped her shoulder, bruising the flesh. 'And what about you, *cariad*? A wife who waits until her husband is a thousand miles away across the Atlantic before she slips into a West End nursing home to have his baby scraped out of her. I'd say that was pretty cruel—wouldn't you? Or was I simply never intended to know?'

She could hear the words, but they made no sense. Gethyn's dark face, poised above her to swoop and plunder, was suddenly a blur. The firelit walls were closing in, the ceiling descending and the floor, in some crazy way, tilting up as if to receive her limp body, as she slipped sideways to the ground at his feet and lay still.

It was the sound that was familiar in some strange way, she found herself thinking. That steady rather metallic tapping —if only she could remember what it was. Her eyes opened slowly and unwillingly.

She didn't remember the ceiling. That was quite certain. She'd never seen those heavy beams and steeply sloping roof anywhere before. And it was a strange bed that she was lying on—an old-fashioned wooden bedstead, and a mattress that was hard without being uncomfortable. Strange bedclothes too. A sleeping bag, and a single sleeping bag at that.

But at least she knew what the sound was now. After all,

she had lain in bed many times listening to it. It was the
sound of Gethyn typing. Only he wasn't in the next room.
If she turned her head very slightly, she could see him, sitting with his back to her only a few feet away at a small
table.

She gave her head a bewildered little shake. Where was
she, and why was she there? And what was Gethyn doing,
working at his typewriter while she lay here in this sleeping
bag, swaddled like a baby? ... A baby.

Memory came flooding back to lash at her, to awaken
her to full and agonised consciousness. Gethyn hated her
because he believed she had deliberately got rid of the
baby—their baby. He had brought her there to punish her,
and soon he would get up from the table and come across
to this bed and take her with that same hatred in his
heart. And if he succeeded in his avowed aim and made her
pregnant, she would always have that hatred to remember
—while she was carrying the child and after it was born.
And what hope was there for any of them?

Moving with utmost stealth, she managed to lower the
zip on the sleeping bag a little way. At least she was still
fully dressed. There was no way in which she could have
managed to put her clothes on noiselessly and get down
the stairs in the corner without him hearing her. Whereas
now she did have a chance—a remote one—of making a
dash for it while he was so absorbed in his work. Slowly, by
inches, she managed to extricate herself from the sleeping
bag, her eyes fixed on his back. The tiny sound she did make
would surely be drowned by the noise of the typewriter
keys.

In spite of herself, she could not help wondering what he
was writing. It must be very important to him if he could
lose himself in it to the exclusion of everything else. Whatever it was, if she managed to get away from the mill, she
would owe it a debt of gratitude.

A questing foot discovered her shoes, but she made no
attempt to put them on. She picked them up and tucked
them under her arm. Stockinged feet would be best to carry
her the few feet to the head of the wooden staircase.

She crept across the room, wincing slightly at the rough-nes of the boards under her feet, and keeping a wary eye on Gethyn. But her luck seemed to be in. He did not falter in his task, or make any attempt to turn and look at the bed. Nor did he seem to hear across the room the thunderous beating of her heart.

She could still feel the dampness of tears on her face and taste their salt on her lips. And there was no one to dry them but herself. After the things he had said to her—the accusation he had made—she had nothing to hope for from Gethyn. He was ready to believe that she had deliber-ately destroyed their child, and yet he was the one who had talked about trust. But at least it explained the silence of the past two years.

She was about halfway down when the stair under her foot gave a resounding creak. Above her head, she heard Gethyn swear, and the sound of his chair scraping across the floor, and panicked, trying to rush the last few stairs, desperately trying to gain the ground floor and the friendly darkness only a few yards away.

She felt her foot slide on the wooden surface and herself plunge forward, catching unavailingly at the rickety hand-rail. Her shoes went flying out of her hand as she hit the ground, falling not heavily, but awkwardly, her arm trap-ped underneath her.

'God in heaven!' Gethyn came racing down the stairs and knelt beside her. 'What are you trying to do, you crazy little fool—break your neck? Here, let me help you. Have you hurt yourself?'

'I'm quite all right,' she snapped. She was scared and winded, but that was all, surely? She got up gingerly on to her knees, then pushed herself up on to her feet. Gethyn rose too and looked at her with narrowed eyes.

'Let me see your arm.'

'I've told you—I'm perfectly all right,' she insisted almost wildly. She couldn't let him touch her after what had just passed between them. That would be past all bearing.

'Move your fingers,' he ordered shortly.

Reluctantly she obeyed. 'Satisfied?'

'Not entirely. Pull your sleeve up. I want to see if there's a swelling.'

She didn't want to. For one thing she was just becoming aware, now that the first shock had worn off, that her arm was indeed very painful. But that was natural, wasn't it? After all, she had just banged it on a hard floor. But the pain should be getting easier all the time, she thought, and yet there seemed to be no way in which she could hold her arm and make it comfortable even.

Biting her lip, she pulled back her sleeve and extended her arm almost defiantly. His fingers moved on her skin, featherlight, and she yelped involuntarily.

'So it does hurt.' There was a sort of grim satisfaction in his voice.

'Of course it does. I've bruised it,' she said defiantly. She brought her other hand up underneath to support it, and it felt infinitesimally better. 'I tell you I'm all right,' she added, her voice rising.

'You're far from all right,' he said flatly. 'Sit down on the step and I'll put your shoes on for you.'

'I can manage my own damned shoes!'

'Fine,' he said with heavy sarcasm. 'Let's see you do it, then.'

There was sweat beading her brow by the time she had got one of them on and the laces weren't even tied. She heard Gethyn curse under his breath, then he seized her other foot roughly, thrusting the shoe on to it and knotting the laces with an almost savage twist.

'Come on,' he said, putting his hand under her good arm and urging her to her feet. 'We have a fair old drive ahead of us.'

'Where are we going?' She hung back, staring at him, her eyes wide and apprehensive.

'To a hospital that has a casualty department,' he said shortly. 'They don't grow on trees in this part of Wales, I'm afraid.'

'You're being ridiculous!'

'I don't think so.' She was being led now inexorably towards the door which had been her original goal, and the irony of this did not escape her. 'You may have bruised your arm as you say, or you may have sprained it. Whatever you've done, an X-ray will tell us all about it. Wait a minute.' He caught up his coat from the table and felt in one of the pockets, producing the headscarf she had bought in Dolgellau. His mouth twisted as he looked at it. 'Perhaps we can find a use for this abomination after all.'

Davina stood numb with fury while he fashioned a rough sling and put her arm into it.

'Please take me back to Plas Gwyn,' she pleaded when he had finished. 'Your aunt could put a cold compress on it for me and . . .'

'Don't argue,' he said, and doused the lamp.

The air outside felt chilly as he put her into the Land-rover.

'You're in for an uncomfortable time until we get on to the road,' he informed her. 'If you start to feel sick just hang out of the window.'

She wasn't sick, but she could have been, and faintness was threatening to overwhelm her again by the time the jolting ceased and they emerged mercifully on to the road. She made herself sit up, carefully avoiding moving her arm which was throbbing dully and persistently, and took a grip on herself.

Gethyn did not speak, and in the dim light inside the Landrover, the lines of his face seemed to show strain.

It was she at last who broke the silence between them. 'I don't recognise this road.'

'No. We're going to Aberystwyth. It's fractionally nearer.' His voice sounded almost impatient. But more than that— worried, as if he was actually concerned about her. But that was hardly possible, she thought with a bitter little twist to her lips. It was far more likely that he was regret-ting the loss of his night's entertainment.

At length he glanced at her. 'Are you warm enough? These aren't the most comfortable of vehicles, as you've already found out to your cost this evening.'

'I'm quite all right,' she lied. 'I think this mercy dash of yours is simply carrying things to extremes.'

'Perhaps.' She was aware of the jut of his chin in the darkness. 'But I'm taking no chances.'

The dark folded shadows of the hills seemed to close them round as they drove. Occasionally Davina spotted the twinkling lights of a farmhouse set back off the road. Nothing overtook them. Gethyn was driving as if he meant it, but other cars swooped towards them, their lights like bright searching eyes. She found she was closing her eyes involuntarily against the unwanted brilliance, and at last she dozed a little.

When she opened her eyes, the road had widened, and there were houses and street lights, and Gethyn was swinging to the right, putting the Landrover at a long, steep hill, and the large brilliantly lit building which stood at its crest.

He held the glass doors open for her to pass into the casualty department. It seemed almost deserted. A young man in a white coat doing a crossword puzzle lowered his paper and gave Davina a searchingly professional glance as she was escorted to the reception desk. The formalities completed, a young bearded male nurse led her along a passage to a curtained cubicle.

'Hurting, is it?' He peered at her arm inside the sling, and gave a slight whistle. 'Don't answer that. I can see for myself.'

The doctor's fingers were firm but gentle as they explored the swollen area just above her wrist. Like an automaton Davina moved her fingers on instruction, and had to bite back a cry of pain when she attempted to move her thumb.

'Hm.' The doctor looked across at Gethyn with a slight grimace. 'One definite fracture and a possible scaphoid as well. But we'll know more about that when we see the X-rays.'

The young man with the crossword puzzle turned out to be the radiographer, and Davina made herself sit very still, trying not to flinch as he arranged her injured arm in all kinds of positions for the camera.

Gethyn was waiting when she emerged from the X-ray room.

'I've found you a cup of tea,' he said briefly, handing her a paper cup. 'Hot and plenty of sugar. Good for shock.'

She was quite glad to sit down beside him on the bench in the reception area and sip her tea. It was quite revoltingly sweet, but after a while the quaking feeling in the pit of her stomach began to dissipate, and she began to feel considerably more human.

In what seemed like no time at all she was back in the cubicle hearing the bad news. Two fractures—one just above her wrist and another at the base of her thumb. She couldn't believe it. She'd had far worse falls than the one she had just suffered. She had fallen off ponies as a child, and on the ski slopes when she grew older, and had never been a penny the worse from any of them. She'd stood more chance of hurting herself that afternoon when she'd scrambled round the rocks to find the dragon's cave.

She sat numbly watching the dripping strips of plaster being expertly applied round her hand and thumb. Her right hand, she thought desolately. It would have to be her right hand. What was she going to do now? How was she going to drive her car? Her arm was not hurting so much, she had to admit, now that it was supported by the plaster, but it felt as if it did not belong to her, swathed in plaster almost from her elbow to her knuckles. She wanted very badly to find a quiet corner somewhere where she could sit and cry until there were no more tears, but no one seemed prepared to let her do that.

She found herself meekly accepting a list of instructions about how to look after her arm, and then Gethyn, his hand warm under her other arm, was shepherding her back to the car park.

He gave her a brief look as he climbed in beside her. 'How do you feel?'

'I don't know.' She stared down at her arm. 'I can't quite believe all this has happened. I feel such a fool.'

'I broke a collarbone playing rugby one season,' he said. 'And I broke this'—he tapped his nose—'the next. I gave up rugby after that. Too bloody dangerous.'

She knew he was trying to make her laugh and was

grateful for the sudden lightening of the atmosphere.

'What position did you play?'

'Full back,' he returned casually.

She pondered her scanty knowledge of rugby. 'Oh—like J. P. R. Williams.'

He gave her a faint grin. 'I wouldn't put myself quite in that class.'

'I had no idea you played rugby,' she said casually, and could have kicked herself.

'No.' His brows rose sardonically. 'But then it was never the past you were particularly interested in, was it, *cariad*? Only the present, and the future, though there was damned little of that as it turned out.'

'I'm sorry,' she mumbled.

'Don't be.' He sighed harshly and explosively. 'There's little point now. Perhaps if we both get out of this mess older and a little wiser, it will have served its purpose. Who knows?'

There was tension between them again now—almost tangible, and she regretted it. Just for a few fleeting moments they seemed to have recaptured the easy comradeship of their courting days, the companionship which had so often and so easily turned to passionate need, one for the other. At times, she thought unhappily, they could be walking, laughing at some mutual nonsense, hand in hand like children. Then the next moment they would be in each other's arms, man and woman completely. Oh, where had it gone? Why had she let it go?

She stole a sideways glance at Gethyn under her lashes and saw that he was frowning faintly, his fingers drumming restlessly on the steering wheel as he drove. They were out of Aberystwyth now. The sea was behind them and they were heading inland, back to the tall hills. She moved restlessly. The little drama was over now, and they were back to the major event. Because she'd been injured and frightened, a lot of things had remained unsaid. But there were other things—other statements that had been brought out into the open, and these were what rankled.

She remembered everything he had said before her faint-

ing fit with a deadly clarity. She had been too hurt, too bewildered at the time to reason it all out, but now she had
nothing else to do but stare ahead of her through the windscreen and brood, and she did not like the conclusions that
were buzzing like a swarm of angry bees inside her brain.
When Gethyn had first launched his bitter tirade, she had
assumed that he believed she had miscarried on purpose—
thrown herself down the stairs, perhaps. There was a bitter
irony in that now.

Yet now she knew that he believed there had been nothing careless or accidental in the loss of the child. That
somehow, even without his consent, she had managed to
wangle herself an abortion. But how could he think such a
thing? True, at the time he had been on the other side of
the Atlantic, but her message to him, begging him to come,
telling him what had happened, had surely been clear
enough?

Unless it had not been delivered properly. Out of the
nightmare of pain and fear, she could remember one thing
clearly. Her mother—cool and elegant as always—at her
bedside, wiping her forehead with a dampened cloth. Her
voice quietly soothing. 'My darling—my poor little girl.'
And her own faltering reply: 'Tell Gethyn—ask him to
come.'

But what had her mother told him? Davina felt a shiver
run down her spine as she tried to come to terms with this
new possibility. Mrs Greer had hated Gethyn and resented
her marriage and every aspect of it. Her concern for Davina
had been real, but her attitude afterwards made it clear that
she thought her daughter should be glad she had not been
made to bear Gethyn's child. And she had not bothered
to conceal her relief and pleasure when Davina told her
quietly she intended to write to Gethyn telling him she did
not want to see him again.

Davina had assumed at the time that her mother's relief
was simply at the marriage being at an end, but now she
wondered if it was not quite as simple as that. If Mrs Greer
had another even more potent reason for wanting her
daughter and hated son-in-law kept at a permanent

distance. If she had lied ... Davina flinched away from the thought, but it had to be faced. If she had told Gethyn a deliberate lie, then that was all the reason in the world for not wanting him to return to London to check up on what she had said.

She sank her teeth into her lower lip. Was her mother really capable of such deliberate malice? she wondered dazedly. She was a selfish woman and a spoiled one, but no worse than that, surely? She could be ruthless—with weak bridge opponents, with friends who proved broken reeds. There was little compassion in her, as Davina had always been aware. She was icy-brained over money too, and her successful dealings on the stock market were a legend in her intimate circle. And she hated Gethyn, and all he represented.

And people whom Vanessa Greer had reason to dislike were cut out of her life without mercy, or the right to appeal. Davina had seen it happen a dozen times and been appalled. One day, someone might offend. The next, they seemed to have ceased to exist as far as her mother was concerned.

She came back to the present with a start, aware that they were turning off the road.

'Are we back so soon?'

'We're nowhere near back,' he returned. 'I think you've had as much as you can take for one night, so we're going to stay the night here, if they have a vacancy.'

She opened her mouth to protest, but the Landrover had stopped and he was already climbing out, and walking up to the front door of the house.

Davina closed her eyes and leaned back against the seat. Was she to be spared nothing? she wondered wearily. She could only pray that their potential landlady would not have a vacancy or that she would not like the look of them and send them on their way. After a brief conference at the door, Gethyn came round to the passenger side and opened the door.

'Down you get,' he directed curtly. 'There is a room. I've told her what's happened, and she's gone to heat up some milk and find you some aspirin. I told her you were bushed.'

'Can't we go back to Plas Gwyn?' She looked at him pleadingly. He'd said 'a room', not 'rooms'. Did he still intend, in spite of everything, to carry out his threat? Her eyes searched his face, but there was no hint to be gained from his enigmatic look, as he stood implacably waiting to help her out, not even bothering to answer her question. He had made the decision. All that was left for her was to obey it.

Her head bowed defeatedly, she let him help her down and walked across the small gravelled space to the front door. There was a small vestibule, crowded with folding chairs and a cheerful huddle of buckets and spades, and a small square hall beyond.

As they waited, a door from the back of the house opened and their hostess, a round dark-eyed robin of a woman, appeared carrying a tray.

'There now.' Her gaze took in Davina's white face and shadowed eyes and the plaster cast on her arm with an all-encompassing thoroughness. 'You poor girl! A warm drink and bed, that's what you need. This way.'

There was no choice perforce but to follow her. Davina was acutely aware of Gethyn following behind her, his body almost brushing hers as they ascended the narrow stairs. It was a large room at the back, with large furniture to match, and the double bed with its blue candlewick bedspread took pride of place.

'Shall I fetch you a hot water bottle?' Their hostess set the tray down on the bedside table and smoothed the bedcovers with a proprietorial hand. 'Then I'll bid you goodnight,' she added as Davina refused the offer with an effort at a smile.

It seemed very quiet in the room once the door had closed behind her. Davina stared down at the flowered carpet.

'We could do with some air.' Gethyn walked over to the window and gave the top sash an abrupt jerk. Then he drew the curtains. Immediately the room seemed to close in on them, become more intimate.

'Do you want to get into bed before you have your milk?'
He opened the bottle of aspirin, and shook a couple into his
palm, before turning to see why she had not replied. The
expression on her face must have been totally revealing,
because he swore coldly and comprehensively and then
walked over to her.

'What are you imagining now?' His voice sounded icy
with fury. 'That my foul lusts have to be satisfied before
all other considerations? Considerations like ordinary
decency? Contrary to your expectations, *cariad*, I have not
brought you here to rape you. You have my word on that—
not that I expect it to count much with you. You're here
simply because I think you need a rest. If they'd suggested
keeping you overnight at Bronglais, I'd have welcomed it.
Understood?'

She nodded faintly, hot tears pricking at her eyelids.
'I'm sorry,' she managed.

'So you keep saying.' He turned away with an impatient shrug. 'Let's take all the apologies as read, shall
we? It would be much less complicated.'

'I suppose it would.' Her tone sounded ragged, and she
hoped he had not noticed. She walked over to the bed and
sank down on the edge, reaching for the beaker of milk. She
took the aspirin he passed her without argument, wishing
only that they could numb the ache in her heart as effici-
ently as they would disperse the throb in her arm. She
wanted oblivion, yet everywhere she looked, he seemed to
be. When she had drunk the milk, he took the beaker and
replaced it on the tray, then squatted down in front of her
looking up into her face.

'I suggest,' he said quietly, 'that you'll be more comfortable out of your sweater and jeans. I also suggest that you'll
find it well-nigh impossible to get out of them unaided at
first. If you want, I'll call Mrs Evans back, or I could help
you myself. Which is it to be?'

She hesitated painfully, aware of an odd wistfulness deep
inside her. Then she said almost inaudibly, 'Help me—
please.'

He was very gentle as he eased the sleeve of her sweater

over the plaster. She could almost have said tender, but
such a word had no place in their relationship. His attitude
was reassuringly matter-of-fact as he tugged the garment
over her head and tossed it on to the bed. Then he undid
the button on her jeans and lowered the zip, guiding the
fabric over her hips.

'Step out,' he ordered briefly, and her jeans went to join
the sweater. He reached behind her and turned back the
bedcovers. 'We'll leave it at that, I think. From what
remember, you're not in the habit of sleeping nude.'

'No,' she said, cursing inwardly at the faint colour that
rose in her face.

He rearranged the pillows slightly. 'That's better. The
doctor said you ought to keep your arm raised slightly for
tonight at least. Get in.'

Davina compiled, wriggling until she could find a position in which she might be able to get some rest. The cast
on her arm wasn't particularly heavy, but it felt incredibly
bulky and obtrusive as she tried to get comfortable. She did
not look at him, but she could hear the rustle of his clothes
as he removed them, and then the bed beside her creaked
under his weight.

'Gethyn,' she said, her throat suddenly tight.

'I'm sorry, Davina.' His own tone was flat. 'But not even
for you am I prepared to spend a cold night in that travesty
of a fireside chair. I won't touch you, I give you my word,
no matter what I may have implied earlier today. Now, go
to sleep.' He switched off the bedside light, plunging the
room into darkness.

She lay very still. It was better this way, she told herself
blankly. Far better that he should think that she had been
registering an instinctive protest about his unwanted presence in her bed than that he should guess the shameful
truth. For the fact was that she had welcomed his unfamiliar weight and warmth beside her. And more than
welcomed. Wanted to feel him not just beside her but
against her, pressing her down into the softness of the
mattress—his mouth, his hands exploring, uncovering . . .

She turned away almost convulsively towards the edge of the bed.

'Davina.' His voice came softly through the darkness, and she tensed. 'I just wanted you to know if it's any comfort to you that I agree to the divorce. When we get back to Plas Gwyn, I'll sign anything you want. You don't have to worry any more.'

She felt him turn away from her, towards his edge of the bed. She didn't move, but her brain was teeming. It was totally ludicrous, she thought. For him to say that, at this of all moments! As she lay here barely two feet away from him, longing for him, hungering for him as if the past had been wiped out. But why was that so impossible anyway? she asked herself. If you loved someone, surely the love went on no matter how deep the hurt, or how long the parting. And she did love him. There was no more room for doubt. Loved him and wanted him too, until her teeth ached with it.

But he didn't want her. Oh, he might have taken her in a spirit of revenge, but it would have been on a strictly temporary basis. His anger against her had died now, stifled by pity for her weakness maybe, and all that remained in its ashes was indifference. That was why he had vetoed apologies and explanations. Because he had been looking ahead to their ultimate parting, and wanted to make it as simple as possible. A clean break.

She caught the edging on the pillowslip between her teeth and gripped it tightly to prevent herself from moaning. How hard she had fought all this time to conceal the truth, most of all from herself. And how hard she was going to have to fight still if she was to get out of this situation with even the remnants of her pride left intact.

She shut her eyes so tightly that brightly coloured specks danced and jigged behind her eyelids, imagining what it would have been like, what she would have felt if she had offered herself to him, and he had refused.

Somehow she would have to get back to London and proceed with the divorce, and hope that eventually she

would be able to exorcise him from her mind, her heart
the innermost recesses of her soul. Perhaps, she thought
that was all she had ever been afraid of—the knowledge o
the depth of her commitment to him. It was true that she
had been spoiled all her life in material things, but rea
love, real caring had for the most part been strangers to
her. Mrs Greer's main concern was that Davina should be
credit to her. When she was being a submissive daughter
then she was treated amiably. Uncle Philip, she knew, ha
genuine affection for her, but his prime concern was with
his own family and she would not have had it otherwise. No
wonder she had been overwhelmed by what Gethyn could
so effortlessly make her feel! But once again she had bee
cheated. He had only the hollowness of passion to offer her
not the warm reassurance of loving that she needed.

Forgetting that she was not alone, she gave a long dee
sigh, and started as he spoke.

'Can't you sleep? Is your arm paining you?'

'A little.' It was only half a lie, she placated her con
science. She had to stifle a little cry as his hand touche
her bare arm.

'No wonder you can't sleep,' he said roughly. 'You'r
half frozen. Why didn't you take that hot water bottle sh
offered you?'

'I think I must still be suffering from shock.' Her voic
shook a little. 'I—I can't seem to get warm.'

She heard him give a muffled groan, then the bedspring
creaked as he moved. His arm went round her and she wa
drawn back against him, folded tightly into the curve of hi
body, absorbing his warmth.

'Better?' he asked drily.

'Yes.' She could barely manage the whispered mono
syllable. His closeness, the knowledge that unlike hersel
he had no hang-ups about sleeping nude, were playin
havoc with her senses.

Gethyn sighed and muttered something she could no
catch, but she did not dare ask him to repeat it. She mad
herself lie like a stone, forced her breathing to become dee
and regular, wanting to deceive him that she had falle

asleep. And gradually, in spite of herself, fiction became
fact, and she slipped almost without realising it over the
edge of drowsiness into slumber.

She woke with a start. It was still early, but daylight was
edging into the room through the curtains. She found they
had changed their positions in the night. Gethyn now was
lying on his back, and she was lying with her head on his
shoulder and her good arm flung possessively across his
bare chest.

She knew what had woken her. Her right shoulder felt
cramped from the unnatural position her broken arm had
got into. Moving carefully so as not to wake Gethyn, she
moved her arm to a more reasonable level, and eased her
shoulder ruefully. It was encouraging to find that her arm
hardly hurt at all this morning, and there was no sign of
swelling or discoloration in her fingers.

She was thankful she had woken first. It was one thing
for Gethyn to keep her warm in the night, but quite another
for him to wake up and find her draped all round him. Not
that he wasn't perfectly capable of extricating himself
from the situation if he was so minded, she thought
bitterly, recalling how he had left her bed without waking
her on the day he left for America, and she had fallen asleep
wrapped in his arms only a few hours previously.

She sat up warily and glanced at her wristwatch. It was
just past seven a.m. She turned and looked down at him.
He looked much younger when he was asleep. The harshness seemed wiped magically from his face. Almost as if he
was conscious of her regard, he stirred suddenly and muttered something. She bent closer, frowning a little as she
tried to catch the words, and heard, '*Rydw i eisiau cusan.*'
Whatever that meant. She straightened hurriedly as his eyelids flickered and opened.

'Good morning,' he said lazily. He lifted his hands and
raked them through his dark hair. 'And how is your arm
this beautiful morning?'

'Fine,' she replied huskily. She was only too aware of his
potent attraction. The tan on his shoulders and chest

looked darker still against the white sheets. His hair was
tousled and the green eyes were lazily warm as they looked
at her. Davina felt the silence between them fill with all
kinds of tensions. She could feel her heart beating with a
slow languor. Her lips parted soundlessly and she moistened them with the tip of her tongue.

Gethyn sat up with sudden briskness. 'Well, that makes
good hearing. I'll be getting up now. We don't want to
make too late a start.'

'But it's still early. What time is breakfast?' Davina
heard herself protest lamely, and blushed.

'I haven't the faintest idea, but if I get up, no doubt I
can find out.' Gethyn spoke with studied patience. The
warmth in his eyes had faded, and he looked edgy.

Davina shrugged rather sulkily. 'Just as you please. If
you're sure Mrs Evans won't mind you roaming around
downstairs before the house is awake.'

Gethyn exhaled deeply.

'Davina,' he said with ominous calm, 'if you know what's
good for you, you won't argue any more. I'm trying—none
too subtly, I admit—to get out of this bed, and out of this
room as well, come to that.'

'Well, don't let me stop you.' Davina hunched a shoulder
irritably.

He swore under his breath. '*Duw*, girl, don't you see
that's exactly what you are doing? Even with your arm in
plaster and that—act of vandalism you had perpetrated on
your hair, you're still so lovely that you tear at my guts.
And in a minute you're going to ask me to help you get
dressed.' He swore again and began to push back the
covers.

'You talk in your sleep,' she told his back as he sat on
the edge of the bed and reached for his jeans.

'Only talk?' he enquired derisively. 'I'm surprised I don't
gibber and foam at the mouth.'

'What did you say?'

He threw her a look over his shoulder and she flushed
again at the idiocy of the question. 'It was in Welsh,' she
mumbled, staring down at the bedspread.

'Well, at least I have that much sense. If everyone sleep-talked in a different language, it would probably save a hell of a lot of recriminations in the morning,' he said drily.

'Please tell me what you said. I can remember what it sounded like.' Haltingly she repeated the musical syllables. Gethyn was very still suddenly. Then he gave a brief un-amused laugh.

'Said that, did I? I must have been having sweet dreams. I wish I could remember them. It means, *anwylwyd*, "I want a kiss." '

Without pausing to question the wisdom of her action, she leaned across and pressed her lips to his brown, muscular back, halfway down his spine.

He turned slowly and looked down at her. Davina leaned back against the pillow and laughed up at him, but there was no answering amusement in his face.

'What the hell do you think you're playing at?' he said very evenly. 'Have you any idea of the risk you're running— of how close I came just now to breaking my word to you? I promised not to touch you, and you're not making it easy for me, Davina.'

'And you're not making it easy for me either.' She was aware of the provocative picture she must make in the brief lacy bra that barely covered her breasts.

He said very softly, 'Then let's make it easy for both of us.' He swung himself back on to the bed, and lay only inches away from her, his eyes burning into hers. She tried to steady her suddenly ragged breathing, but it was im-possible. He put out a finger and gently stroked the curve of her cheek, the lobe of her ear and the long smooth line of her throat. And paused.

'Haven't you something to say to me?' he murmured. 'You were fluent enough a moment ago.'

He repeated the syllables with her under his breath, smiling a little as she stumbled in her eagerness to be word perfect.

'*Rydw i eisiau cusan*, Gethyn,' she whispered at last. Her eyes shone at him and her lips parted tremulously. 'Oh, darling, *rydw i eisiau cusan*.'

Her plea was forgotten as his lips met hers with a fierce seeking wonder, and she responded without reserve. Her uninjured arm went up to clasp his neck and her fingers tangled in his hair as she held him to her. His mouth caressed her eyes, her ears, her throat before returning over and over again to her lips as if he would drain their sweetness dry. His hands moved on her, caressing her with passionate longing, removing the final frail barriers to his desire.

There was not an inch of her body that he did not explore with intimate awareness, arousing her to a need as great as his own.

At last he lifted himself over her, his eyes fierce as a dragon's as he stared down at the glow, the sheer wanton invitation of her.

'Oh, God, I love you, Davina,' he said hoarsely. 'Tell me you love me, *cariad*, even if it isn't true. Say that you want me.'

She thought that her heart would burst with her joy.

'My love, my own . . .' Her voice broke as she welcomed him to her.

Afterwards as she lay at peace in his arms, she murmured, 'What was that you were saying about a divorce . . .?'

'A divorce?' He frowned teasingly, pretending to try and remember. He bent and kissed one of the soft strands of hair straying across her forehead. 'Do you really think I'd let you go now, *anwylyd*?'

She put up a hand and stroked his cheek. 'You need a shave.'

'For that I need a razor.' His mouth met hers lingeringly. 'And my razors are all at Plas Gwyn. I'll phone Aunt Beth and tell her to throw a few things in a suitcase for us. We'll collect them on our way.'

'On our way where?'

He shrugged. 'On our honeymoon. Does it matter where?' He smacked the curve of her hip lightly. 'Up with you, wench, and I'll get you reluctantly back into your clothes.'

'I'm sure I can manage,' she protested. 'Get dressed and go and make your phone call.'

It was more of a struggle dressing one-handed than she realised, but at last she was decent at least. She didn't put on her shoes because she was nervous of the dangling laces, but carried them in her good hand.

She was humming a lighthearted little tune as she crossed the landing and went down the stairs. Gethyn was below her in the hall, still talking on the telephone. His back was turned to her, but she knew by his sudden rigidity that something was wrong.

She halted halfway down the stairs, watching as he replaced the receiver and turned slowly to meet her.

He was a stranger again, cool and watchful. The passionate lover who had caressed and taken her to the edge of rapture and beyond might never have existed.

'Gethyn?' Her eyes were troubled as they returned his gaze. 'Is—is something wrong?'

He looked her over. 'So you did manage,' he commented levelly. 'In the circumstances that's just as well.'

She tried to laugh. 'All is not what it seems. I couldn't manage my bra hook. Or these.' She held her shoes towards him with a little pleading gesture.

He did not move. 'Just as well,' he repeated as if she had not spoken. 'It seems our honeymoon will have to be cancelled after all, *cariad*. You have a visitor awaiting your return to Plas Gwyn.'

'A visitor?' she said stupidly. 'But I'm not expecting anyone.'

His lip curled. 'No? That's not the impression she gave Aunt Beth when she arrived late yesterday evening. Raised Cain, apparently, because you weren't there to make your obeisance. Seems to think you want rescuing and taking back to London under her maternal wing.'

'Oh, no,' she said faintly.

'Oh, yes, Davina.' There was a savage note in his voice. 'Mummy's turned up trumps for you once again, *cariad*. And don't try and pretend you didn't have it all arranged between you before you ever came to Plas Gwyn. Well, I give you full marks for duplicity, Davina. Your acting has improved beyond recognition. But don't you think last night's—performance was carrying things just a little too far?'

He turned on his heel and walked off, leaving her standing there on the stairs, motionless.

CHAPTER EIGHT

THE drive back to Plas Gwyn was a nightmare. They set off almost at once, forgoing all the offers of breakfast which a bewildered Mrs Evans tried to press upon them. Davina could not be sorry. Apart from the physical handicap of trying to feed herself one-handed, she knew she would not have been able to force a morsel past her dry throat.

She was totally bemused by this new turn of events. To pass in one brief hour from the heights of ecstasy to despair again was more than she could bear. She felt drained of life as she sat beside Gethyn in the Landrover, staring out at the rich sunshine which so poorly reflected her own mood.

She had tried to plead with Gethyn, to convince him that her mother's arrival was a complete shock, but to no avail. He had accepted her assurances with an overtly cynical contempt which cut her to the quick. But it was clear that he regarded Mrs Greer's descent on Plas Gwyn as part of a carefully prearranged plot to extricate Davina from any possible consequences of her reckless action in coming to Wales. No doubt his aunt had also told him about her phone call to London, although neither of them knew that it had been totally unsuccessful. She supposed her mother must already have been on her way to Wales by that time.

At first Davina had been tempted to dig her heels in and refuse to return to Plas Gwyn at all. But in a way that would simply have been another form of the running away Gethyn had previously accused her of. She had to face her mother and convince her that her interference in her life was both unwelcome and unnecessary. At the same time, she had to find out the truth about what had actually transpired while she was ill in hospital, no matter how unpleasant these revelations might be.

She stole a sidelong glance at Gethyn. His dark face looked intractable, his mouth set in a grim line, his brows drawn together. He had not looked at her or spoken a word since they had set off, and this new barrier between them was an agony to her when she recalled the total intimacy they had enjoyed together only a short while before.

Somehow she had to find a means of re-creating that emotion, the sense of giving and sharing that had bound them so passionately together. Last night she had wondered desperately how she was to salvage her pride. Now in the clear light of day, pride seemed to have very little relevance. She wanted Gethyn, and she wanted his trust and support.

'Gethyn.' Her voice was very quiet and shook a little. 'We—we must talk. We can't let everything slide like this —not after last night.'

'Why not?' He did not even trouble to take his eyes off the road for a second. 'We enjoyed a pleasant interlude together, and now it's over and you can get back to your safe, tidy life in London as you always planned.'

'How can you say that?' she whispered. 'It wasn't like that. You know it wasn't. Oh, how can I make you believe me?'

'You don't have to. Just for a while, abstinence made your heart grow fonder, and I let myself be fooled into thinking it could last. But it couldn't. Nothing ever does.'

'Love lasts,' she said steadily. 'And you said you loved me. Didn't you mean it?'

He gave a slight shrug. 'No doubt I meant it at the time,' he said callously. 'Men are prone to exaggerate at such moments, as you must know. You're not that naïve, Davina.'

'That's the cruellest thing you've ever said to me,' she said in a low voice.

'Then thank your stars you won't be around much longer.' He pulled out to overtake a lorry with unerring precision. 'Go back where you belong, *cariad*. Time heals all wounds, they tell me. The sort of scratch you've just suffered shouldn't take long at all. Get Mummy to kiss it better.'

She turned her head away and stared out of the window

with unseeing, tear-blurred eyes. Her nerves were stretched almost to screaming point by the time they swung on to the Plas Gwyn track, but in a way the coming confrontation would almost be a relief.

As they reached the parking spot, Davina saw the Fenton family gathered round their car, packing luggage and equipment into the boot. They waved cheerfully as the Landrover bumped past, and Davina forced herself to return the greeting.

When the Landrover stopped in front of the house, she sat very still for a moment, fighting for her self-control. She was tempted to ask Gethyn for her handbag, still under the tarpaulin in the back. She wanted a mirror so that she could check there were no too obvious signs of distress, and repair what ravages there were with a touch of concealing powder and lipstick. But there was little point in such tactics, she told herself. Her mother would be quite capable of seeing through the kind of pitiful façade she would be able to assemble.

She climbed down and walked with a steadiness that amazed her up the path to the front door. Her heart was beating uncomfortably as she crossed the threshold, but the only person in the hall was Tim Fenton, unnaturally neat and tidy, who was lingering by the dining room door. His face lit up when he saw her.

'Gosh!' His eyes widened as they discovered her arm. 'What have you done?'

'Broken it, I'm afraid.'

'Oh.' He looked downcast. 'I was hoping we could go on a dragon hunt before I left. We're going this morning, did you know?'

'Yes.' She smiled down at him with an effort. 'I knew. Have a safe journey. And it's far too early for a dragon hunt, anyway. The lazy beasts don't wake up until around lunchtime,' she added, trying to alleviate his obvious disappointment.

He sighed. 'I only wanted to say goodbye to it,' he muttered half-resentfully.

'Say goodbye to the horses instead. I daresay Mrs Parry

would give you some carrot for them, if you asked her. Now I must go, Tim. Someone's waiting for me.'

She crossed to the sitting room and opened the door. Her instinct had been quite right. Mrs Greer was sitting alone on one of the sofas, smoking a cigarette with quick jerky movements, an untouched cup of coffee on a low table in front of her. She looked up irritably as Davina entered. 'At last——' she began, then gasped. 'My God, what have you done to yourself?'

'I broke my arm in a fall. Didn't Mrs Parry tell you . . .'

'Not that.' Mrs Greer dismissed Davina's injury with an impatient wave of her cigarette. 'Your hair—your general appearance. I cannot believe what I see. In less than forty-eight hours you've turned yourself into a scarecrow!'

Davina ran a hand through her hair with irritation. 'Did you come all this way, Mother, just to criticise the way I look?'

'Of course not.' Mrs Greer leaned back against the cushions, her mouth set in a thin line. 'I telephoned here yesterday morning to find out when you would be returning. The woman who seems to run this place informed me you had gone out—with your husband—and that she didn't know when you would be back.'

'I see.' Davina pulled a leather-covered pouffe forward and sat down on it. 'And following on that information, you felt obliged to drive all the way here. Did you drive, by the way? I didn't see your car anywhere.'

'I hired a car,' Mrs Greer returned almost absently. 'It will be returning for me in about an hour. I hope you can be ready by then. Have you a dress or something you can put on?'

'Oh, yes,' Davina said calmly. 'But you've had a wasted journey, I'm afraid. I have no intention of leaving here.'

There was a long silence, during which Mrs Greer studied her daughter with narrowed eyes.

'I don't think, Davina,' she said at last, 'that you quite appreciate my concern for you. Have you any conception of what I went through last night—arriving here, only to find you were still with that man, and that no one seemed to have any idea of your whereabouts?'

'Perhaps you were the only one who considered that it was any of your business.' Davina raised her eyebrows and saw her mother flush angrily.

'Please don't be insolent or try to be clever,' she snapped. 'You may have been married, Davina, and have found yourself a career of sorts, but you're still a child in many ways. You told me you were coming here to get a divorce. That was the only reason I agreed to permit it . . .'

'Mother.' Davina leaned forward, her eyes fixed earnestly on the older woman's face. 'Please believe me when I say you no longer have the right to give or refuse me permission to do anything—particularly where my marriage is concerned.'

Mrs Greer's smile was thin and angry. 'So it's like that! This is just what I was afraid of. You never had the least sense of proportion where that man was concerned. He's always been able to exert this—animal influence over you. It nauseates me even to think about it. What a fool you are, Davina! He treats you like dirt, and you crawl back to his feet when he snaps his fingers, like a whipped dog.'

'I love him,' Davina said quietly.

'Love?' Mrs Greer invested the word with an almost strident mockery. 'What you feel for Gethyn Lloyd, my dear, is very far removed from love. You're sexually infatuated with him, and he proved when he left you how much of a lasting bond that kind of thing is. I didn't bring you up, Davina, to be used by a man like that.'

'What do you know of Gethyn?' Davina got to her feet and walked over to the window. 'Only your own prejudices.'

'Well, one would hardly call him a responsible pillar of society.' Mrs Greer gave a little silvery laugh. 'I suppose I must admit to being prejudiced against a man who deliberately abandons my daughter at such a time. I defy any mother to feel differently.'

Davina turned and looked down at her mother. 'I see. And it was this same spirit of maternal concern, no doubt, that made you tell him I was having an abortion.'

The colour faded from Mrs Greer's cheeks with startling suddenness, leaving two ugly patches of rouge standing out starkly on her cheekbones. She made an immediate recovery, but for Davina it was enough. She had seen the truth written on her mother's face, and she felt sick inside.

'Is that what he's told you? Oh, my darling!' The appalled tone sounded really sincere. 'He misunderstood me completely—or else he's deliberately out to make mischief. He always was jealous of our relationship. I knew that from the first.'

'No, I don't think he's out to make mischief. And I can't think how anyone could get words like miscarriage and abortion muddled.'

Mrs Greer moistened her delicately reddened lips. 'But that's exactly how it happened, darling. I remember now. I didn't say "miscarriage". I used the clinical term, which the Sister told me. I said you were having a "spontaneous abortion". He can't have heard me properly. It wasn't a very good line.'

'It still isn't,' Davina said bleakly. 'And what about the rest of my message to him? Was that also translated into clinical terms? Such as "You've done enough harm. Get out of her life and stay out" instead of "Please come. She needs you." Is that the way it was?'

'I admit nothing, you understand.' Mrs Greer was on her feet now, her eyes blazing. 'But believe this—anything I did, I would do again. He's not the man for you. Look at this house.' She gave her surroundings a derisive glance. 'Does he really intend to bury you in this dead and alive hole? Oh, God, Davina, think before it's too late. Come back to London with me. When you're free, you can do anything you want. One day you'll meet a decent man from your own background, someone who will treat you with the sort of consideration every woman wants. In a couple of years you'll inherit the money from your father's estate. You'll be quite a wealthy young woman. I don't know whether you're aware of that . . .'

'Oh, yes, quite aware.' Davina gave her mother a searching look. 'And perhaps I'm not the only one. Is that it,

Mother—the reason for all this maternal devotion? Father's money? But you don't need it. You have money of your own. Or have you had some losses over the past year or two that I don't know about?'

'You're being ridiculous and insulting, but I'll overlook it this time because you're obviously upset.' Mrs Greer picked up her handbag. 'You don't understand a thing about the stock market. You never have done.'

'I have a feeling that once Father's money became mine, I might have been given a chance to learn,' Davina said drily. 'But not, of course, if I was still married to Gethyn. As my husband he would have been entitled to a major say in how the money should be used. But not, of course, if we were divorced.'

'I refuse to listen to another word.' Mrs Greer walked to the door. 'I am more distressed than I can say. I'm going outside now to wait for my car. I expect you to join me. I'm sure in spite of the hasty things you have said, the totally unwarranted accusations you have made, that you still realise where your best interests lie.'

When the door had shut behind her, Davina sank down on to a chair and closed her eyes. Well, at least now she knew the truth, unpalatable as it had proved. And she had kept from her mother the satisfaction of knowing that her intervention had been just as disastrous as she could have wished. She gave a long and bitter sigh. Was that really all there had been behind the heartache and misery she had suffered? Her mother's instant realisation that Gethyn was not the kind of son-in-law who could be manipulated and used for her own ends? It had not been merely chemistry that had set her at odds with him, but the knowledge that his shrewdness and will would be pitted against hers once he was Davina's husband.

Davina felt sick. It gave her no satisfaction to realise that it was her mother's own too casual reference to her inheritance which had set her on the right track at last. It was a measure of Mrs Greer's desperation that she should have made such a mistake. She wondered almost dispassionately just how much money her mother had lost in the economic recession. She would never know, of course.

Her mother had urged her to leave Plas Gwyn and go back to London before it was too late. There was a strange irony in that. If she did ever return to London, it would be because it was too late.

Mrs Greer would never admit anything, so there was no point in involving her in a confrontation with Gethyn. Somehow she would have to find the means to convince him herself. But how? She shivered at the memory of his rejection of her arguments earlier.

She went slowly out of the room and up the stairs to the bedroom. Mrs Parry was there, re-making the bed with fresh linen.

'I had to put your mam in here last night, see. I knew you wouldn't mind, and there was nowhere else. She seemed very upset that you weren't here, even though I told her you'd come to no harm with your man with you.' She sighed. 'I asked her to stay for lunch, but she will have it she must get back. Is she going to bring that car all the way down the track to fetch her again?'

'I would imagine so,' Davina said rather drily. 'Walking any distance is not one of her pastimes.'

'There now.' Mrs Parry's eyes widened. 'And how's your poor arm?'

Davina glanced at it. 'I haven't given it a great deal of thought so far this morning, so it must be all right.'

'How did you do it?' Mrs Parry shook open a pillowcase and began to insert the pillow.

'Didn't Gethyn tell you?' Davina raised her eyebrows. 'I thought you were in his confidence.'

'I wouldn't say that.' Mrs Parry laid the pillow on the bed, frowning slightly. 'He wouldn't thank me for putting my nose too much in his affairs, good as he is. He told me he was taking you to spend a few nights up at the old mill cottage or I'd have been worried, but he doesn't say a lot about his plans.'

'I see.' Davina hesitated for a moment. 'I had a slight accident on the cottage stairs.'

'What a shame!' Mrs Parry gave the plaster an indignant

look. 'Spoiling your second honeymoon like that.'

Davina turned away. 'I would hardly have described it in those terms,' she muttered.

'Well, that was what Gethyn called it. Wanted to get you on your own, he said, and talk it all out.'

'He said that?' Davina stared at her, conscious of the stirring of a sudden hope. 'Aunt Beth, you don't know where he is, do you? I—I'd like to have a word with him.'

'He's not here. He's gone round to Huw Morgan's to return the Landrover and collect his own.'

'I see.' Davina subsided, disappointed again. 'You've no idea when he'll be back, I suppose?'

'None.' Mrs Parry smoothed the blankets into place. 'Although he did say not to expect him back for supper.' She gave her wristwatch a distracted glance. 'Oh, dear, I'm all behind this morning.' She hurried away, muttering.

Acting with sudden decision, Davina grabbed her suitcase. She couldn't pack anything properly, but tumbled her possessions in, one on top of the other, pressing them down ruthlessly with her left hand. She opened the drawers in the dressing chest and took out some of Gethyn's sweaters and underwear, adding them to the things already in the case before going along to the bathroom and finding his razor and shaving soap in the wall cabinet. She didn't think she'd forgotten anything, but if she had they would just have to improvise, she told herself with more optimism than she had felt all day.

Getting the overstuffed case shut with only one arm proved a more difficult matter, and she was struggling with it, swearing under her breath, when a voice spoke from the doorway.

'Packing?' It was Rhiannon.

'Spying?' Davina returned.

The other girl flushed and came forward into the room. 'No, I'm not,' she retorted. 'I'm looking for that little nuisance Tim Fenton. His family are all waiting to go and there's no sign of him.'

'I think you'll find he's in the stable giving the horses some farewell carrots.'

'Indeed he's not. That's where I looked first. Here, let me do that.' Rhiannon took the case from her and forced it shut.

'Speeding the departing guest?' Davina asked with open sarcasm.

'Well, you don't expect me to weep over you, do you?' Rhiannon said defensively. 'I could have made Gethyn forget all about you in time. I know I could.' She sighed. 'Well, I can't stand here arguing. I have that kid to find.' She gave Davina a curious look. 'What made you think he'd be with the horses?'

'Something he said downstairs. He was hanging about in the hall when I came in.'

'Hm.' Rhiannon pursed her lips. 'I wonder if Gethyn saw him?'

'Well, he had the Landrover at the gate . . .' Davina paused as a thought occurred to her. She flushed slightly. 'I suppose Tim wouldn't have climbed into the back of the Landrover without Gethyn seeing and gone joy-riding over to Morgans' farm?'

Rhiannon stared at her. 'Why should he do that? Mucky old way to ride, that.'

'Precisely,' Davina said rather dryly. 'It struck me it's the sort of thing a kid might do.' And some supposed adults, she added silently.

'I'll give Huw a ring,' Rhiannon decided. 'It's worth a try, I suppose. I hope you're right in a way, because his mam's getting anxious about him.'

She went out, and after a pause to make sure she hadn't left anything, Davina followed her. There was quite a council of war gathered in the hall below. Mrs Parry was there, looking more harassed than ever, but attempting to allay the fears of Mrs Fenton, who was sitting on the hall chair looking rather pale. Even her mother had joined the group, Davina noticed with faint surprise. As she came down the stairs, Rhiannon returned to the hall.

'He's not there,' she reported briefly. 'But Huw's coming over to help us look.'

'God help him when we do find him,' Mr Fenton said

grimly. 'He's too fond of roaming off like this. He never sees the slightest danger in anything.'

Mrs Greer detached herself from the group and came over to where Davina was standing.

'What an unfortunate thing to happen,' she said in a tone of complete indifference. 'I suppose one can hardly blame the Parrys, but it is to be hoped that the child will be found safe for their sakes. Are you ready, Davina? The car is here. I told the driver to give us five minutes.'

'I'm not going with you, Mother,' Davina said patiently. 'I couldn't leave now anyway even if I wanted—not with Tim missing. If there's going to be a search party I want to help.'

'With a broken arm? You'll be a complete liability,' Mrs Greer said scathingly. 'Don't get involved. After all, these people mean nothing to you, Come along, Davina. I can't keep the driver waiting any longer.'

'Then go,' Davina said, quite gently. 'You see, Mother, I am involved for better or worse. This is Gethyn's home, and I'm his wife.'

Mrs Greer's eyes were inimical as they met Davina's. She gave a short mirthless laugh. 'Then I wish you joy of it, my dear, and of your husband's garrulous aunt, and that sulky daughter of hers. I hope you won't have too many regrets.' She turned away. Davina followed.

'I'll see you to the car.'

Mrs Greer did not reply. Her back very upright, she swept down the path towards the gate. At the gate, she stopped.

'You needn't come any further,' she said dismissively. 'You've made your decision, and I don't suppose I shall see you again. I hope you'll have the courtesy to tell your uncle what you've decided. Though no doubt he will encourage you. He always did have a soft spot for Gethyn Lloyd—that "Welsh fire-eater", as he called him.' Her smile was pure ice. 'I hope you don't get scorched by the flames, Davina. Goodbye.'

She did not make any attempt to embrace Davina or touch her at all. She climbed into the back of the car and motioned the long-suffering driver to be on his way. Davina watched the car lurch uncomfortably up to the first bend in the track, then turned to go back in the house. Then she stopped, remembering what her mother had just said. 'A fire-eater,' she thought. 'A dragon. And Tim talked about the dragon. He wanted to go up to the cave to say good-bye.' A feeling of chill settled in the pit of her stomach as she remembered the deep pool and the slippery rocks. Quite safe when there were adults around to keep a watchful eye. But for a small boy on his own? She had taken one step towards the house when she heard the sound of a vehicle and turned back eagerly, hoping it might be Gethyn. But it was Huw Morgan's cheerful face smiling at her over the steering wheel.

'Don't look so stricken, *bach*,' he greeted her as he jumped out. 'The kid won't have got far.'

'He might—and I can't help feeling I'm partly to blame.' Swiftly she told him of Tim's preoccupation with the dragon story and her own lighthearted encouragement. 'I practically told him there was a dragon,' she ended tragically. 'Oh, Huw, if anything's happened to him, I'll never forgive myself!'

Huw glanced at his watch. 'And when did you see him in the hall? Come on then, let's put your mind at rest. He won't have got that far, if that's where he's heading. I'll take the Landrover for part of the way, to save time. Get in.'

Davina sat beside him, hunched forward a little, her eyes scanning the distant horizon for a small figure. Huw glanced at her. 'Relax! You're like a cat on hot bricks. It's not just the disappearance of young Master Fenton that's upsetting you, is it?'

'No,' she said.

He sighed. 'I suppose it's you and Gethyn again. Oh, hell and damnation! I really thought things were going to work out for you after last night. I was telling myself I'd done the right thing when I phoned him and told him you'd suddenly arrived out of the blue.'

'You phoned him?' Davina stared at him. 'But I thought it was Gethyn's aunt.'

'No, it was me. I had a nasty feeling you might just vanish again if I didn't do something drastic.'

'And was that why you took me out dancing?' Davina enquired dryly.

He reddened a little. 'Only partly. And I did tell Gethyn.'

'I wish you'd told Mrs Parry. She started regarding me as the scarlet woman.'

He grinned. 'I think she'd regard any girl I took out apart from Rhiannon in that light.'

'How are things now—between you and Rhiannon?' asked Davina.

Huw shrugged lightly. 'Static, you could say. But I'll win through in the end, have no fear.'

Davina regarded him with amused wonderment. 'I believe you.'

'And up on the hill,' said Huw with great satisfaction, 'is boyo.'

He stopped the Landrover and they got out. Huw put his hands to his mouth and bellowed Tim's name, but the distant speck went on climbing steadily away from him.

Huw hesitated. 'I'll go and get him,' he said. 'Will you wait here for me?'

'I think I'll follow slowly.'

'Well, mind the old arm,' Huw warned solicitously as he loped off up the slope. 'One bit in plaster at a time's quite enough!'

Davina found herself smiling as she followed his flying figure at a sedate pace. She had no real reason to feel sorry for Rhiannon, she thought. Rhiannon had it made.

It was even warmer on the hill than it had been the previous day, and the flies were persistent and annoying. It was quite a relief to sink down on the grass and watch for Huw returning, a protesting red-faced Tim hoisted on his shoulders.

'It's not fair!' he was saying loudly as they came within earshot. 'It's nearly dinner time and the dragon would have woken up by now.'

'Then that's just the time to keep out of his way,' Huw returned. 'And your mam's worried sick about you. If you don't consider other people's feelings, then you don't even deserve to see a dragon.'

He dumped Tim on to the front seat and turned to Davina. 'Jump in, *bach*, and I'll run you both back.'

Davina hesitated. In the distance she could see the jumble of grey stone and slate that was the mill and its out-buildings and an idea had occurred to her.

'I don't think I'll go back yet.' She smiled at Huw. 'I feel like a stroll.'

'All right, then.' He gave her a dubious look. 'But don't go overdoing things. We don't want any more accidents— or searches,' he added, aiming a playful swipe at a down-cast Tim, plainly contemplating the wrath to come.

Davina meekly promised to take every care and stood watching as the Landrover swayed and lurched down the track towards Plas Gwyn and out of sight. Then she turned and continued up the valley towards the mill.

It was the first time she had seen it in daylight. It was a tall rather narrow building, the long windows revealing that it was built on three storeys. Beside it a huge wheel turned slowly but powerfully in the creaming water. It was very quiet apart from the sound of the water and the coo-ing of pigeons somewhere nearby. Davina shaded her eyes and stared up at the windows, but there was no sign of movement. It seemed that the renovation work was not being carried out today for some reason. The adjoining buildings, including the cottage she had been brought to the previous night, looked almost derelict in comparison, although it was clear that remedial work was being carried out on them too. The one nearest the mill, she guessed, was going to be the mill shop that Mrs Parry had mentioned, and she wondered what plans Gethyn had for the other— apart from using it as a makeshift love nest, she thought with a wry smile.

She trod up to the cottage door and knocked tentatively, but there was no reply or sound of movement within. After a while, she lifted the latch and walked in. Everything was just as it had been left the night before—the half-unpacked roll of bedding, coffee mugs dumped on the table, and dead ashes in the hearth. Last night the place had had a cosy, if rather seedy, charm. Today, it simply looked neglected. Davina compressed her lips. If it had not been for her arm, she thought wistfully ... Yet there were some minor improvements she could make, notwithstanding.

She searched round until she found a small handbrush and an ancient shovel and set herself to clear out the grate; dumping the feathery wood ash into an old cardboard box. Then she rinsed the coffee mugs under the single cold tap in the corner.

She wandered round the cottage, opening any windows that seemed strong enough to withstand her handling. Then she carried the bedding up the stairs, making several journeys. She would have liked to have made up the bed, but decided it would probably be beyond her. Besides, there was plenty of time for that.

She was just deciding that her efforts deserved a cup of coffee when she spotted the table and the typewriter in the corner. She stared at it for a moment, her instinctive curiosity battling with her respect for Gethyn's privacy. But curiosity won. Why had he told her he was doing no more writing, when it was patently untrue? she wondered. Was it possible that the business proposition from Uncle Philip had prompted him to start again? Somehow she did not think so.

There were a number of sheets of paper littering the small table, and a thick wad of manuscript inside a cardboard folder. Guiltily, Davina opened the folder and peeped at the top sheet. She flushed slightly. It wasn't a novel at all. It appeared to be some kind of diary, and she had absolutely no right to be snooping there at all. She was just about to close the folder when her own name seemed to leap out at her from the closely typewritten page.

She bit her lip. It suddenly seemed totally imperative that she should discover what Gethyn had written about her. With a sense of shock, she realised that the papers in the folder were dated two years previously—in the period just after their marriage and before Gethyn had gone to the States. With a feeling of incredulity, she realised that it must have been this diary, and not the novel she had thought, that Gethyn had been engaged on night after night as she had lain awake listening to the clatter of the type-writer.

She sat down on the chair and began to read at first in silence, but then aloud as the sense and meaning of the words in front of her began to come home to her. It was not merely a diary that Gethyn had written during those long nights. It was more a love letter—a long, articulate but passionate outpouring of a man't deepest feelings. And it was also, she discovered as she read bewilderedly on a portrait of herself.

Nothing was hidden. His longing for her and her love was revealed over and over again in passages of lyrical tenderness. But his own self-loathing and doubts were also frankly discussed—his hatred of the travesty of passion he had forced on her on their wedding night—his determination to wait for her to come to him in her own time even if it took the rest of their lives. Every word she had spoken to him during those weeks in the flat, every emotion however fleeting she had expressed, each time she had smiled—everything was there in those close-packed pages.

'My angel and my demon,' he had written at one point. 'Sometimes I am tempted to risk everything by telling her how much I love her and need her. Yet I know it would be cruel to burden her like that when it is so plain she cannot return my feelings. I have to face the fact that she may never do so, and why should I make her suffer more than I have done already by allowing her to see my suffering?'

Oh, Gethyn, she thought, her throat aching with threatened tears. If only you had obeyed that impulse and told me—how different everything might have been. Yet at the same time she could understand and honour the reasoning behind his self-imposed restraint.

His stated intention—to lead her slowly and gently from the heady delights of their courtship days to the deep relationship that marriage would demand—had been defeated by her own sudden intransigence.

She fumbled the sheets back into the folder, blinded by

tears. All those wasted hours, days, weeks when they could have been lovers instead of strangers, forging a bond so strong that no malice however calculated could have come between them. Whereas, separated by circumstances, a prey to their own uncertainties, they had proved easy victims.

Her hand reached out for the new sheets—the pages he had typed, presumably since her reappearance in his life— then hesitated. She was frightened. Supposing they did not contain the reassurance she longed for?

She got up and went over to the bed and lay down, pulling the sleeping bag over herself. She felt cold suddenly. No written words, however evocative, could warm her now. She wanted the strength and passion of Gethyn's arms around her, his lips setting fire on fire. Or was it too late, after all?

She never knew when, worn out by crying and the emotional debate she was waging with herself, she fell asleep, but when she woke again she realised that several hours must have passed. The sun had moved round and was now falling directly across the bed itself, and she found her forehead was beaded with perspiration. She sat up, pushing her damp hair back from her face, wondering what it was that had woken her. Then she heard the sound of movement in the room below and her heart began to thump slowly and agonisingly.

She slipped noiselessly off the bed and tiptoed to the head of the stairs, peering down into the room below. All kinds of possibilities were flashing through her mind—that it might not be Gethyn at all, but one of the workmen concerned with the mill—or that Gethyn might not have come alone.

But he was there and quite alone, sitting at the kitchen table, his back turned towards the stairs. As she watched, he slowly lowered his head on to his folded arms and became very still.

Davina came down the stairs very carefully, clutching at the rail with her left hand.

'Gethyn,' she whispered.

His head came up immediately, and he swung round on

the chair, scraping its legs across the floor. He looked haggard and ill, and his chin was dark with stubble. For a moment he stared at her as if he did not believe his eyes, then, as if some internal shutter had been operated, his face became cold and closed.

'Davina?' he said flatly. 'What the hell are you doing here? You should be halfway to London by now.'

She shook her head. 'What made you think that?'

'You went with her,' he said tiredly. 'They told me so at the house. What happened? Some last-minute change of heart? Or is Mummy here too?'

She descended the remaining stairs and came towards him. 'She's not here, Gethyn. She's on her way back to London. But I didn't go with her.'

He shook his head, as if he was finding it hard to concentrate suddenly.

'Well, you should have done,' he muttered. 'There's nothing here for you.'

'You're here.'

'But not for very much longer.' His lip curled. 'Have you forgotten I'm setting out on my travels again? I rang your uncle earlier and told him the good news, and he seemed delighted. I shouldn't be surprised if you get a bonus when you return to London. In addition to the divorce, that is.'

'That isn't what I want.'

He shrugged cynically. 'Then that's your tough luck.'

'I do have alternative proposals.' She knelt beside his chair looking up into his face. 'Don't you want to hear them?'

'No,' he said. 'And for God's sake get up. That floor must be filthy, and the time when I would have rejoiced to see you grovelling at my feet is long gone.'

She smiled. 'If I'd had the use of both hands, I'd have cleaned the floor. I did do the dishes and the hearth.'

'So I noticed. I hope you don't expect me to be grateful. My domestic arrangements here might not go down very well in Knightsbridge, but they suit me very well and I can do without your interference or anyone else's. Now why don't you push off back to Plas Gwyn like a good girl, and phone your mother and resolve whatever tiff you've had with her, and then leave. Perhaps then we'll all be happy.'

'I can't phone my mother, Gethyn,' she said steadily. 'Perhaps one day I shall be able to forgive her for what she tried to do to us—what she did do. But not yet.'

'Now what are you saying?' His mouth twisted sceptically.

'I'm talking about the lies she told you when she telephoned you in America. The reason I didn't follow you on the next plane that day was because she was ill—some kind of virus. I nursed her through it. She was convalescing when I had a fall—down the stairs at the house.' She tried to smile. 'But I didn't get off so lightly that time. I'd have welcomed two broken bones. Instead I started to lose our baby. They took me into hospital and did everything they could, but it was no use. I asked someone to contact you, to get you to come home and be with me, but my mother—intervened. Someone—a nurse—had told her that the clinical term for miscarriage was "spontaneous abortion" and she deliberately used those words and twisted them to make you think that I hadn't wanted the baby, that I'd deliberately got rid of it. But it wasn't true, Gethyn. I wanted your child then, just as I wanted you. Just as I want you now.'

'No.' He shook his head. 'You never really wanted me. Oh, you came to me. You let me take you—make love to you. But afterwards you cried, and I knew that you regretted what you had done. That was why I left like I did. I couldn't bear to look into your eyes and see you hating me. And when your mother phoned, I knew I'd been right all along.'

'But you were wrong,' she said quietly. 'Just as you were wrong not to tell me that you loved me from the first. Why didn't you?'

'You were so young, you frightened me sometimes. I was afraid you weren't emotionally ready for the demands I might make of you,' he answered, then paused, his eyes narrowing. He looked down into her suddenly flushed face, then glanced towards the stairs and the upper room. 'I see.'

He gave a mirthless laugh. 'Well, I wouldn't pay too much heed to those maudlin ramblings, *cariad*. They don't stand the test of time.'

'I don't believe you,' she said. 'Oh, Gethyn, darling Gethyn, I just don't believe you.'

He remained motionless for a moment, then with a stifled curse he got up and went over to the window and stood staring out.

'Go back to London, Davina. That's where you belong, no matter what your mother may have done.'

'I belong with you.' She went on kneeling where she was. 'I belong to you. I've been deceiving myself for so long, telling myself I hated you, that I never wanted to see you again. Yet as soon as I was given the opportunity, I came to you. Oh, I may have told myself that it was to ask for a divorce, but deep inside——' she shook her head. 'I think I always knew what the outcome would be.'

'And what will it be?' His voice was very hushed suddenly.

She smiled and got to her feet. 'It's too early to say. But who knows? You might have to chain me to your wrist for the next nine months, after all.'

She only took one step towards him. He came more, much more than halfway to meet her, lifting her off the ground into the strength of his embrace, crushing her mouth under his. His face was remorseful when he released her.

'God, *anwylwd*, your arm! I haven't hurt you, have I?'

'What are you suggesting? That I should keep you at arm's length for the next six weeks?' The eyes that she lifted to his face were alive with love and laughter.

'Heaven forbid!' He drew her close again, his lips exploring hers with total possessiveness. Then he picked her up bodily and carried her over to the rocking chair, seating himself with her curled on his lap. 'I have a confession to make to you, Davina.'

'Is it about Rhiannon?' she asked, her heart beating faster. 'If it is, I'd much rather not know.'

He swore. 'It is not about Rhiannon. She happens to be

my cousin and a nice, though rather mixed-up kid. But I don't love her and I never had the slightest intention of marrying her.'

'But you said . . .'

'No, you jumped to a conclusion, *cariad*. I said my wife-to-be was still rather young. And so you are, my darling heart. You were my wife, Davina, even when we were miles apart. There was never room in my life for anyone else.'

'Is that the confession?'

'No.' He hesitated. 'That involves someone else—your uncle, as a matter of fact. I've been in touch with him on and off for about a year now. I made no secret of the fact that I still loved you and wanted you back, and I knew he was on my side. There is a new book, *cariad*, though it's still in my head as yet, and the American tour was broached months ago. He thought he might be able to use it somehow to bring us together—and you played right into his hands.'

'You pair of fiends!' She pummelled at his chest with her clenched fist and Gethyn captured it laughing and carried it to his lips. His eyes were warm and sensuous as they looked into hers and she felt the answering tide of a desire she had no longer any need or reason to conceal beginning to sweep over her.

'This place,' he murmured, 'is far from being the ideal honeymoon retreat. It's spartan to say the least and its mod. cons. are neither modern nor particularly convenient. On the other hand, we shall be alone here, which we wouldn't be at Plas Gwyn.' He paused. 'I bought Plas Gwyn for you, *anwylyd*, and for our children, but it's Rhiannon's home too until she marries, and Aunt Beth's. Will you mind too much?'

'I don't know,' she told him honestly. 'But don't let's create difficulties before they arise. As long as I have you, everything else is unimportant.'

'You have me.' His mouth rested on hers with an eternal pledge. 'And at last my love, my wife, I have you.'

Titles available this month in the Mills & Boon ROMANCE Series

THE JEWELLED CAFTAN *by Margaret Pargeter*
On holiday in Morocco, Rosalind Lindsay found herself in the hands of a sinister bunch of Nomads. She was rescued — but was her mysterious rescuer any better?

REBEL IN LOVE *by Lilian Peake*
Schoolteacher Katrine Hume was determined to fight the powerful Lex Moran over the future of her school — but then she fell in love with him . . .

PHILOMENA'S MIRACLE *by Betty Neels*
Philomena happily accepted a job in Holland if it meant seeing more of attractive Doctor Walle van der Tacx — but he was to marry the lovely Tritia!

THE WILDERNESS TRAIL *by Kay Thorpe*
Regan loved Cal Garrard, but it was fairly obvious that he didn't return her feeling. And when Regan met his beautiful stepmother, she realised why . . .

NEW MAN AT CEDAR HILLS *by Elizabeth Graham*
'I don't need a man,' declared Abby Mackenzie. Nevertheless, she found herself relying more and more on her new ranch foreman, Ben Franklin.

DRAGON'S LAIR *by Sara Craven*
Davina and Gethyn's marriage had been brief and disastrous, but now, after two years, they had been thrown together again, and Davina's feelings for her husband were stronger than ever!

THE VINES IN SPLENDOUR *by Helen Bianchin*
Shannon's life wasn't made any easier by the presence of Nick Stanich. He knew she didn't like him — so why couldn't he leave her alone?

CONFLICT IN PARADISE *by Sally Wentworth*
Tansy had to stop Major Blake Aston from making her paradise island home an army fuel base — but how?

OPEN NOT THE DOOR *by Katrina Britt*
All Laraine got for her pains in caring for the crippled Moira Frazer was to fall hopelessly in love with Charles McGreyfarne — the man Moira was going to marry!

NOW OR NEVER *by Anne Weale*
Beautiful Annabel's whole affluent world crumbled on her father's death, but she was told there was one obvious thing she could do — approach the millionaire tycoon Nicolas Casimir!

Mills & Boon Romances
— all that's pleasurable in Romantic Reading
Available August 1978 — Only 50p each

Also available this month
Four Titles in our Mills & Boon
Classics Series

*Specially chosen re-issues of the best in
Romantic Fiction*

August's Titles are:

WAVES OF FIRE
by Anne Hampson

It was five years since Shani had married Andreas Manou —
but the marriage had been in name only and she had not seen
him since the wedding day. And now Shani was planning to
marry again — and Andreas had chosen this moment to come
back into her life . . .

THE WHISPERING GROVE
by Margery Hilton

Cheated of her career as a ballet dancer, Toni made a loveless
marriage with Justin Valmont in the hope that in caring for
his motherless small daughter she would find a new purpose
in living. But she did not foresee the effect on her heart of
Justin's devastating charm — or the return of his old love, the
beautiful Lucy Sandanna . . . .

LOVE AND DOCTOR FORREST
by Rachel Lindsay

It was Philip Redwood's contemptuous attitude towards
women doctors that had made Lesley Forrest throw up nursing
and become a doctor herself. She had never expected to meet
Philip again — but she did, and this time she fell in love with
him; too late, for by now he was married to another woman.

THE MAN FROM BAHL BAHLA
by Margaret Way

To take her mind off the tragic death of her father, Corinne
went to work in Queensland. There she met cattle owner
Kiall Ballantine, who thought Corinne a society orchid and
misinterpreted the reason for her unhappiness. It was the
beginning of a tempestuous relationship.

Mills & Boon Classics
— all that's great in Romantic Reading!

BUY THEM TODAY only 50p